MARRIED TO THE SEAL

HERO FORCE BOOK FOUR

AMY GAMET

1

The only thing Mason Petrovich liked better than setting a bomb had been fucking the president's daughter. And that had been setting a bomb, too, if you thought about it. A political one.

Except she took nine months to detonate.

She gave birth already, but they were keeping the explosion under wraps as best they could. He chuckled. You couldn't keep explosions under wraps for long.

He smiled, looking forward to the culmination of his work. He spliced the ignition wires, twisting in the detonator. They were attacking the president from all sides, and Petrovich couldn't wait to see the flames.

Voices approached in the distance, echoing off the bridge surface, and he froze, his eyes darting from the unfinished circuit to his planned escape route — a large bush some hundred yards off the walkway. He was deep enough in shadow that he couldn't be seen, but he had only moments to finish his work and escape before the people walking toward him reached him and the clearly exposed bomb.

It was a race, and he liked races.

Damn, he loved this shit.

He finished the wiring and started the timer on its countdown. "Let's see you hide this one, Vasile."

He turned and jogged quickly to the safety of the dark shrubbery, only stopping to turn back when he reached relative safety.

From his vantage point, he could clearly see the presidential mansion illuminated in the distance. Grace was there. Grace and his child.

Bomb number two.

It was time for him to show them he knew they were there. Time to leverage the power that had taken so long to create.

He pulled out his cell phone. "The bridge is all set. I'm going up on the hill next."

The man's voice on the other end was firm. "We talked about this. We wait until after the bridge."

"It's my kid, and I want to do it now." He hung up the phone and put it back in his pocket. He pulled out his weapon, the black metal gleaming in the last light of dusk.

Damn, it was good to be back.

The Swiss Alps were beautiful, but nothing to compare to this.

President Vasile walked to his study window and looked out over the city, unseeing.

Evil had been in his house.

It had walked through the door and into the bedrooms of those he loved most.

He'd spent the whole night awake, like a ghost of himself, ambling from room to room as if he could stop it from happening again.

He could see the note in his mind's eye as clearly as when he held it in his hands.

BASTARD. DROP OUT.

He knew who was responsible without knowing the perpetrator. Victor Trane would stop at nothing to win the presidential election, even threatening the family of his opponent.

You could drop out.

You don't have to do this.

But he did have to do it. Someone had to keep Trane from power, or the citizens of the country he loved would be the ones to suffer.

Lightning flashed and the view from his window came into focus. It was raining, and people scurried along crowded sidewalks rushing to work or perhaps home after a long day.

He imagined they were hardworking people, their families warm and just a touch shy of financially stable. He knew what that was like. They deserved the best he could do for them. They needed a president who could turn things around.

He frowned. He'd been that man for twenty-six years, taking his country from a fledgling baby to the industrious teenager it was now. Six months ago he was certain he was still that man.

His chest tightened painfully and he reached in his pocket, withdrawing a metal pill vial and putting one of the tiny pills under his tongue.

You won't do anyone any good if you're dead. Not Grace, not Nico, not the people of this country.

Nobody.

His eyes caught on his reflection in the glass, and he felt as if he were staring at his own mortality. The time he had left on this earth was limited. He knew that. He needed to save his people from Trane before the reaper came and ended his own days.

"Please," he whispered, staring at himself. "Just a few months more."

The ticking of the clock on the wall became louder, its sound almost comically pronounced. He let his eyes close.

The pain began to subside, and he sighed with some relief. Too bad the pain of his opponent's offenses would not be so easily diminished.

Someone knocked on the door of his office before pushing it open wide. Only Grace would do that. He stood up straighter as he turned to face her, the babe bundled tightly in her arms surprising him yet again. Would he never get used to seeing his daughter with a child?

Her brows pinched together in the panicked look she inherited from her mother. "Have you found out who did it?" she asked.

He would do anything to protect her, but this time he was powerless to do so. "No."

"What about the surveillance tapes from the security gate?"

"They're missing."

Her eyes opened wide. "The guards were in on it."

"Yes."

"You need to fire them."

"I already have."

She began to pace. "Nico isn't safe here. I'll take him back to Switzerland with me—"

"Then there will be no one to protect you."

"No one is protecting us here!"

"I have a plan to change that."

"Your men can't be trusted. Those tapes disappearing proves it."

"This isn't one of my men." It had pained him to bring in an outsider, but he knew it was necessary. "He's American. A Navy SEAL. He arrives tomorrow afternoon."

"How did you get him here so quickly?"

He lifted his chin. "I made this plan before the intruder got into Nico's room. I hired him to be your husband until the election is through."

She rounded on him, her nostrils flaring. "You did what?"

"You've created quite a mess. A baby out of wedlock is still scandalous here."

"No, Father. It isn't. Only in your mind." She gestured to the tall windows and the people beyond. "No one out there cares whether or not I have a ring on my finger."

He shook his head. "They care more than you think."

"Well then, I guess they'll just have to accept it."

"You know as well as I do, they will do no such thing. The election will be a close race, closer than any before in our history. When the people find out you have a bastard, many will vote for Trane instead."

Her gaze was steely. "Don't call him that."

"That's what they're going to call him. That's why the intruder chose that word. To show us that he knows about Nico and the effect he will have on the campaign."

"The campaign! That's all you care about. When is it going to be enough for you? How many years must you lead this country?"

"If Trane is elected, he will back Russia's bid to take over the country once more. My sources say he's already accepted their deal. He has a majority stake in Parliament, and two of those who disagreed with him have died tragic, unexpected deaths."

He could see the impact of his words registering on her features. She knew what that would mean for the citizens. She had a fine political mind, could have been a politician herself if she had the inclination.

"We have to stop him..."

"Yes, Grace. We have to stop him from obtaining absolute power. We have to stop him from winning this election."

"And you think Nico is going to make that more difficult."

"Nico is going to make that impossible. You've spent too much time abroad. Conservativism is alive and well here. I had the pollsters add a question to last week's phone survey. Sixty-eight percent of those over fifty would not vote for a candidate whose immediate family had children out of wedlock. They consider it to be a sign of moral weakness."

He gestured for her to sit down, noting the high color in her cheeks and how she hesitated before settling in the chair. It was as if they were separated by a thick brick wall, and it struck him they had built it together, piece by piece, since Lenore died.

That wall would not be coming down today.

"You will marry the American. He will keep you and the baby safe and provide you with the husband I need you to have." He glanced at the baby in her arms. "Do we have a deal?"

He watched her face. She was a smart woman who understood her actions had consequences outside of herself.

She would do the right thing, he was nearly sure of it. Only one thing could stand in the way. "Unless you'd rather marry the real father?"

Her head snapped up.

What he wouldn't give to find out who that was.

"We have a deal," she said.

3

---

arry the father of her child?

She would've jumped at the chance to marry her baby's father, would have fallen over her own feet in her haste to the altar, but she didn't know where he was or even if he was alive.

Grace instinctively pulled the baby more tightly to her chest, the pressure on her overly full breasts making her aware she needed to nurse. As if on cue, Nico stirred in her arms, searching for her nipple with his mouth.

She didn't want to nurse the baby here in front of her father. The thought made her feel so alone. The last few days had been difficult.

No, the last few weeks.

In the days since Nico's birth, she had missed her mother more than she would have thought possible. Every time she had a question about how to do something, how to handle a rash or her son's nighttime fussiness, she longed for her mother's sound advice and warm sense of humor.

But her mother wasn't here, hadn't been here in more

than a dozen years, and it hurt to no end that her sweet son would never know his grandmother.

Her hands clutched at her son's little body. She never knew until he was born just how much she could love another person, the purity and intensity of a mother's love. She would do anything for this child, to protect him or make him happy. Anything at all.

She narrowed her eyes. "And this man you hired, he is willing to pretend to be my husband? Or did you fail to mention that little tidbit?"

"Technically, he wouldn't be pretending. We would need the marriage to be legally binding in case the media suspects anything. You will get a divorce after the election is over."

She squeezed her eyes shut. "That's three months from now."

"Yes. Three months of inconvenience for you to give those people out there a better life."

She laughed without humor. "Inconvenience. Marrying someone I don't even know is an inconvenience."

What does it matter now, anyway?

Her heart was already broken, her hopes for the future shattered. Nico's father would never be part of her life again.

"Getting married now won't change the fact I wasn't married when he was born."

"A minor matter of the date. I'll take care of it."

She nodded and stood. "Does he have a name?"

"Matteo Cruz."

"He must be a real winner if he's willing to marry a stranger for a paycheck."

"Or else he's willing to make a sacrifice for the greater good, just like you are."

A pounding on the study door made her jump, and her eyes met her father's, seeing the matching concern there.

"Come in," said her father.

His security advisor walked in. "There's been an explosion on the pedestrian bridge downtown. It's collapsed, sir."

"Any casualties?"

The man's face was gaunt, haunted. "There appear to be hundreds."

4

Matteo had been following the news out of the Republic of Lutsia closely. The election was hotly contested, a tight race between the long-term incumbent, Anton Vasile, and his opponent, Victor Trane. Each was laying the blame for the terrorist attack at his opponent's feet.

When Matteo got in this car at the airport, he'd been surprised to find Vasile's security advisor, General Talia, waiting inside—ostensibly to brief him on the leader's security concerns for his daughter. But it was clear to Matteo the other man was really here to assess him.

"We have no definitive evidence on who blew up the pedestrian bridge," said the advisor.

"I saw the coverage. It was horrible."

"Yes. One hundred forty-five people gone in the blink of an eye, with twenty-two still unaccounted for."

"Have any terror groups taken responsibility?"

The older man fingered the brim of his hat in his lap. "Only one. A group claiming to be in support of Vasile."

"They're trying to make you look bad."

"Yes."

"Or they are telling the truth."

"Are you insinuating President Vasile would plan a deliberate attack on his own people?"

"Someone did."

"Trane's team is the one that did this. They are attempting to stir up unrest among the citizens as a way to show Vasile is incompetent."

"Is he?"

"How dare you suggest such a thing?"

"He's a legend, and one of the most influential leaders of this century. But he's also old. You know as well as I do there is open speculation about his health."

"From the opposition, yes. But not from within his own camp."

"You resent them bringing in an outsider."

"Yes."

Matteo was failing the security advisor's test, and he knew it. The other man's disdain permeated the car like a bad smell.

"Your only responsibility is to protect the president's daughter. You would be wise to keep your political ideations to yourself."

"Why does she need protecting?"

"That's not important."

Matteo leaned forward in his seat. "I need to be in the loop. I need to know what you know."

"These matters are of the highest security clearance."

"And I've been brought in by the highest-ranking security official in this country, who's trusting me with his daughter. Don't you think that warrants some consideration on your part?"

The men faced off. After a beat, the security advisor

looked down at his hat. "Someone broke into the presidential mansion. They gained access to Grace's son's room and left a threatening note."

"What did it say?"

"Bastard."

"You've kept the birth out of the news?"

"Completely."

"Someone knows. How did they compromise the existing security?"

"We don't know. Anyone who could have been responsible for the breach has been let go."

"Which means you have all new people working there. That's dangerous in and of itself. Who's the father?"

"Grace has chosen to keep that information to herself. We can only speculate. Before leaving for Switzerland, she was known to have been dating Mason Petrovich. On the surface he is an upstanding businessman, but our intelligence agency believes he works for Ten Komanda."

"What's that?"

"It loosely translates to *shadow team*. They're a covert organization. Little is known about them, except they work for the highest bidder doing the unimaginable. We believe they are responsible for the explosion that brought on the pedestrian bridge collapse, but we can't prove it."

"You said you didn't know who did it."

"I have been working for the first family my entire career. I've watched Grace grow up from a baby herself." He took a deep breath. "You were right when you said you needed full disclosure to take care of the presidential family. I have decided to give it to you."

"Why?"

The slightest shine on the other man's eyes told Matteo there was real emotion there. He knew General Talia had a long history with the Vasile family. Clearly they were close.

"Because I can't save them myself," said Talia.

"Is Grace aware of Petrovich's associations?"

"No one is privy to Grace's mind except Grace herself."

Matteo looked out the window and tapped his fingers on his knee, his eyes scanning the lush grounds of the Vasile mansion as his mind worked to frame the situation.

He was a kid from the projects, and he'd only seen places like this on TV. Now he was marrying the president of Lutsia's daughter, even though it would be a marriage in name only.

Jax explained Matteo would be required to accompany Grace Vasile in public, but his life behind closed doors would be his own. His presence here would do much to secure the election for Vasile, and Matteo understood the importance of that for world events.

The limousine slowed as they rounded a corner, a massive structure Matteo found difficult to call a home appearing in the distance.

His assignment was simple. Marry Grace Vasile for three months and keep her and her baby safe from harm. He suspected the latter part of that sentence was going to be far more difficult than the first.

He'd only seen one recent picture of her, a grainy shot, clearly taken from a distance. He'd been struck by the sadness in her eyes even more so than her beauty, which was great.

It was a sham, a false marriage. But at the same time, it was legally real. Someday when he met the woman he truly wanted to marry, he would need to explain why he had chosen to do this for Grace.

For her country.

For human liberty.

"There's one more thing," said the general. "I believe there is a mole close to the administration. The pedestrian bridge that was destroyed was going to be mentioned in Vasile's speech tomorrow as an example of things this administration has done to help the people. Before that, an office building in the capital city burned to the ground. It was slated to be the site of a rally focused on job growth."

"Whoever it is wants you to know they are there."

"Exactly. I fear there will be more terrorist attacks. Every time we discuss a venue or a past initiative, I fear for the safety of those at that location."

"What places are you most concerned with right now?"

"The subway system that runs beneath the city, and the baseball fields that were built on the site of an old munitions factory."

"Have you beefed up security at those locations?"

"To the best of my ability, yes. But I don't want the public to suspect we are concerned, either."

"I understand." The idea that this was an ongoing terrorist situation, with a potential mole so close to the president, was alarming. "I appreciate you letting me know."

The car pulled up in front of wide stone steps that led to an ornate front door and portico. The door opened, the first daughter herself appearing in the entranceway.

Grace.

"What's she like?" Matteo asked.

For a moment he thought the other man wasn't going to answer. "Stubborn."

Matteo grinned. If you only had one word with which to describe someone, stubborn wasn't a bad one to choose. At least these months were going to be interesting.

5

Matteo climbed the stairs, his eyes taking her in from head to toe. She wore sandals and shorts, the length of her legs between them golden from the sun and pleasantly curvy. A grass-green tank top creased beneath her folded arms.

Then he got to her face.

She was fair-skinned and freckled, with wary eyes that matched her shirt and seemed to be assessing him just as he was her. She held out her hand. "I'm Grace Vasile."

"Matteo Cruz. It's a pleasure to meet you."

"Are you ready to get hitched?"

The corners of his mouth pulled up into a smile. "I thought I might walk in the door first. Have a glass of water. That kind of thing."

"Suit yourself." She turned back into the house and he followed her, his eyes immediately going to the ornate molding that climbed up the ridiculously high ceilings.

The mansion was more elaborately decorated than he expected, and Grace seemed out of place, like a game piece thrown into the wrong box.

"How much are they paying you?" she asked over her shoulder as she walked.

She didn't beat around the bush, did she? "My regular salary with HERO Force, plus a small bonus for the inconvenience."

She stopped walking and turned to face him. "Inconvenience?"

"That's right."

She harrumphed, but turned and continued walking. She led him through half a dozen rooms, each decorated in a different color with furniture and artwork that screamed old money — and it just kept going.

He let his eyes slip down her back to the rounded cheeks of her derrière. She moved with a perfect blend of feminine sway and royal disdain, and Matteo searched for her scent on the air.

Something flowery and soft, the exact opposite of how she came off. He was intrigued. Who was this woman who found herself in need of a husband?

The information Jax gave him back at headquarters was limited. She had a baby six weeks ago in Switzerland, where she'd been staying for the past year. She left the name of the father blank on the birth certificate and returned home to Lutsia.

"Where are you taking me?" he asked.

"Water." She pushed through a swinging door and held it open for him behind her. They were in a large industrial kitchen, metal counters gleaming in the sunshine. She pulled out a glass and filled it from the faucet before handing it to him. "Here."

"Are you in some kind of hurry?"

"The priest has mass in forty-five minutes."

He narrowed his eyes. "A Catholic priest?"

"Yes."

Oh, shit.

He'd been expecting a justice of the peace or whatever the equivalent government official was in this country. Every Sunday school lesson he'd ever learned lit up in his brain with a flash.

While he rarely went to church, he still considered himself to be a Catholic at heart, and he hoped one day to get married in the Church. That would prove problematic if he had already done so.

"What's the matter?" she asked.

"You can only get married once in the Catholic Church." They didn't recognize divorce, considering the couple still married no matter their legal status.

She shrugged. "So we'll get an annulment."

They wouldn't be having sex, so the marriage wouldn't be consummated and they could get an annulment with a clear conscience after the divorce was final.

"That's true, but it's a lot more complicated than a divorce. A buddy of mine went through it a few years ago."

"Look, if this is something you don't want to do—"

Did he? It certainly made this whole thing a lot more complicated than he was expecting, but he was here to do a job he believed in. "No, it's okay. Really, I'm fine."

"Nothing to it but to do it." She pushed off the counter and again took the lead back through the house.

"You don't sound like you're from here," he said.

"I went to school in New York," she called over her shoulder. "I spent a lot of time in the States with my mother. She was American so we were always going back there to visit."

A high-arched doorway led to an opulent room with red-upholstered couches and a fireplace taller than he was.

A priest stood waiting, with what could only be a Bible in his hands, and Matteo stopped walking.

He looked at Grace. She held herself stiffly. She was all bravado, but underneath she was scared. He imagined she would bolt from the room like a spooked horse if given the opportunity. He offered her his arm and she looked at him warily.

"You don't need to be nice to me. None of this is real, anyway," she said.

Matteo looked from her to the priest and back again. "Looks pretty real to me."

"You know what I mean." Her eyes shifted to the other side of the room and she took in a quick breath. "My father's here."

Matteo's arm was still out, waiting for her, and after a moment she took it. They crossed the room to President Vasile.

"Good afternoon, sir. I am Matteo Cruz."

Vasile's stare went pointedly to their joined arms. "I see you're already in character. Let's get started."

Grace's eyes flicked to his and he saw they were lightly bloodshot. She was trying not to cry, and a wave of sympathy washed over him. If this was hard for him, what must it be like for her?

Women were sentimental about their wedding day. From what he'd heard, some of them thought about it from the time they were little girls.

"Are you okay?" he whispered.

"Nope." She took in a shaking breath. "Let's do this."

Her voice was steely and he decided in that moment he liked her. When most women would have crumbled, she straightened her spine.

The cry of a baby in the distance echoed through the

house and she jerked, her gaze shifting from Matteo to her father and back. "Nico—"

Her father's voice was gruff. "You can go to him when the ceremony is finished."

Matteo could feel her arm shaking, as if she was physically fighting with herself. The baby's wails got louder. "We'll hurry," Matteo said.

"Ladies and gentlemen, we are gathered here today," the priest said.

"Skip that part," she said. "Get to the vows."

"Do you, Grace Louisa Vasile, take Matteo Cruz to be your lawfully wedded husband?"

"I do."

"And do you, Matteo Cruz, take Grace Louisa Vasile to be your lawfully wedded wife?"

"I do."

"Then by the power invested in me by the holy Church and the People's Republic of Lutsia, I now pronounce you husband and wife."

She pulled her arm free of his, turned, and left the room. He was alone with the priest and Grace's father.

The distant cries stopped abruptly and the priest put on his hat. "I hope you have a happy life, despite this rough beginning," he said. "God works in mysterious ways to bring us the people we are meant to have in our lives."

There would be no happy life together for the two of them, but Matteo nodded his head anyway as he wondered what he'd gotten himself into. It was time to get used to lying, that was certain. "I'm sure we will. Thank you."

The president turned to Matteo. "There is a small reception this evening to formally welcome back my daughter and her new husband. I suggest the first thing you do is inform your bride."

"She doesn't know?"

"No. As my employee, you are notably easier to deal with."

He walked away, leaving Matteo standing in a strange room, in a strange house, in a strange country. He spun in a circle, taking it all in. He needed to get the lay of the land, just as soon as he touched base with Grace about the reception.

He headed back through the house in the direction the cries had been coming from. His mind flipped through the last hour, landing on a shot of Grace's red eyes. He wanted to know who had put that sadness there, why her life seemed so difficult.

He chided himself.

Just stay the course.

That's what he had to do. Do his job to help preserve democracy, and get back to the good old U.S. of A.

The beautiful woman he just promised to love and honor till the day he died had very little to do with his objective, and he'd do well to remember that, no matter how striking her eyes were.

6

G race sat in the glider, her baby at her breast. The calming hormones that surged through her bloodstream as her milk let down were a balm to her battered soul.

She was a married woman. It was ridiculous and unbelievable, and the numbness that had kept her feelings at bay throughout the ceremony slunk to the floor like a shadow.

"I'm sorry," she whispered to the otherwise empty room. Tears welled up in her eyes and spilled onto her cheeks. Hell, she wasn't even sure who she was apologizing to.

Her child?

Her lover?

Herself?

Her hold tightened on the baby in her arms. "I'm not sorry for you. I could never be sorry for you." In that moment, she ached for her lover with a physical pain.

She wished he were here, but hadn't she wished that very thing every moment of every day since he disappeared? There must've been some mistake, some misunderstanding, some horribly important reason he'd needed to go. They loved each other.

Of this, she was certain.

But her confidence had been battered by the months that followed, in the moments he had missed, the birth of their baby, and the embarrassment of coming home without him.

Her father's words rang out in her head. *A bastard. That's what everyone else is going to call him.*

And what of her lover? What if he was alive and planned to come to her, only to discover she'd married another man just weeks after his child was born? She looked at her sweet son at her breast and touched his soft hair lightly with her finger. "He would have loved you."

Without Mason in her life, everything else ceased to be important. It didn't matter that she was married to a stranger. The only thing that mattered now was that she had her son and she had done her duty to keep her country safe.

Now she could hunker down and hide inside these walls that had once felt like a prison. Lick her wounds and pray for the healing she feared would never come.

A knock at the door made her sigh, and she reached for a small blanket to cover herself. Her intense desire to be alone would not be so easily satisfied. "Come in."

Matteo stood in the doorway and she took her first good look at him. He was tall, far taller than she, with wide shoulders tapering to slim hips and a white smile that glowed against his caramel-colored skin. She wondered about his heritage. Maybe Latino, maybe something else.

"I'm sorry, do you want some privacy?" he asked.

She bit her lip. "It's okay. Come on in." She gestured toward a chair comically far to her right and held her breath, relieved when he crossed to it and sat down. "What's up?"

"Your father wanted me to let you know there's going to be a reception for us this evening."

"What?" The last thing on earth she felt like doing was showing off her new husband. She couldn't even remember his last name, but her father expected her to introduce him around? To put a smile on her face and pretend for a formal audience?

She was suddenly so tired she couldn't even imagine doing what was being asked of her.

"I'm sorry, Grace. Personally, I would have put it off a few days, but no one asked me for my opinion."

The numbness was back, spreading over her body and brain. She narrowed her eyes. "This charade is so surreal. You could ask me to pretend to be a talking dinosaur and I might find it easier than this."

"Don't make it more complicated than it has to be. We just need to be friends. Couldn't you use a friend?"

She blew out air. "I don't need a friend; I need a savior."

"Why?"

She shook her head. "Never mind." Cold air on her wet nipple made her peek beneath the blanket. The baby was fast asleep, his mouth lightly open and a perfect cupid's bow. But her other breast was hard and full of milk, and she needed him to keep nursing before her engorgement became painful.

Dammit.

She should have been paying attention.

Made him switch sides before he became full. Her breasts were making too much milk, and she had specific instructions on how she needed to feed her baby.

You can't even do that right.

There was another knock at the door.

She cursed under her breath. "Come in."

A woman in a maid's uniform opened the door, her eyes going sheepishly to Matteo. "I'm Trudy, Miss Grace's maid. I understand you two were married in Switzerland. You have my congratulations. I'm so excited for your reception this evening."

Grace felt her heart sink. It had been a long day, perhaps one of the longest in her memory, and the very last thing she felt like doing was being the center of attention in a crowd of people.

And she would have to pretend to care about this man, as if just breathing in and out were not difficult enough today.

"Maybe you could recommend a dress for me to wear," suggested Grace.

The girl's eyes lit. "Oh, I'd love that! Maybe the cream organza, or the aquamarine satin from France."

"Whatever you think is best. Something forgiving, please. My body isn't yet my own."

"Of course, Miss."

The door closed and Grace stared at it. "What are we going to do?" she asked, the idea of the evening ahead weighing on her like a boulder on her back.

"We try to look happy."

Grace picked up the sleeping baby and gently put him in his crib. "And if I'm not up to the task?"

"Then I'll help you."

He sounded sincere and she was grateful this stranger-turned-husband might actually make this situation easier.

She bit her lip as an image popped into her mind. Wedding guests clinking silverware on glasses to get the couple to kiss. She felt her cheeks heat with embarrassment.

"What if they expect us to kiss? They do that at wedding receptions."

"They do."

"We don't even know each other. No offense, but I wasn't planning on kissing you."

"No offense taken. I wasn't planning on kissing you either."

She ran a hand through her hair. "I don't know what my father was thinking. People are going to take one look at us together and know we're completely full of shit."

And then what would happen? She needed her country to believe this was real. Anything that threw her marriage into question could hurt her father's chances of winning the election. With the recent terrorist attacks, he needed every point in the polls he could get.

"Then we'll have to do better," he said.

"What do you suggest?"

"You do want people to believe us, right? Because right now you're acting like you'd rather give up."

"It's important for this country that my father is elected. I'll do what I have to do to make sure that happens."

He moved toward her. "Then you're going to have to try harder to act like you like me. Your body language around me is all wrong. If we were really married, you'd want to stand close to me. Hold my hand. Stuff like that."

The back of her neck was getting hot. "I'm not sure what you're suggesting."

He moved again so he was standing directly in front of her, and her heart began to skip with anxiety.

"I think we should practice," he said.

"What?"

"Being more intimate. We could practice kissing if you're comfortable with that."

She didn't like the sound of that at all. Given that there was zero affection between them, she'd rather kiss a post. "I don't kiss strangers."

He took a step toward her. "What about strangers who just happen to be your husband? Technically speaking, of course."

His eyes were dark, his stare intense, and it made her shake inside. "Especially those."

He held his hands up. "It will make it less awkward when we go downstairs. But if you don't want to, that's fine with me. I don't care either way."

Now she felt stupid. He was right. They would look more like a couple if they acted like one. She rolled her eyes. "Fine. Let's just kiss and get it over with."

"Well, now I feel vulnerable and a little taken for granted."

He was making fun of her. She felt the corners of her mouth curl into a smile despite her desire to stop them. "You're not funny."

"I'm a little funny."

"No, you're not."

"I could be a world-renowned comedian and you wouldn't even know it."

"Will you just kiss me already?"

He cocked his head to the side. "I don't usually kiss women on the first date."

She hit him in the chest with a backhanded slap. "Just kiss me, Matteo!"

7

H e hadn't meant to tease her, but it was so much fun he couldn't seem to help himself. He reached for her, gently putting his hands on her waist, and she jumped.

So much bravado, but she was scared, and the knowledge made him soften toward her. This couldn't be easy. While he'd been hired for a job, this was her real life, and sympathy made him long to help her.

He dipped his head. She was considerably shorter than him, and her body leaned against his as she went up on her tiptoes to reach his mouth. That scent of flowers was back, mixing with something sweet, and his lips touched hers. Her awkwardness felt to Matteo like the nervousness of an inexperienced, tentative lover.

She kisses like a virgin.

Blood surged to his cock at the thought. Of course she was not a virgin. She was a mother, for Christ's sake. A breastfeeding mother with lush, full tits that had turned him on the moment he walked in the room and realized she was nursing.

Don't be a pervert.

He lifted his head just slightly, enough to break their kiss, but her eyes blinked open and he saw desire there. She wanted him to kiss her again.

Matteo froze.

If he did, it would affect their relationship for the whole time he was here. This was a job, after all, and it wouldn't be right for him to go beyond what was required.

But he couldn't seem to make himself step back. Her cheeks flushed a deep crimson and she dropped her head.

His hand was at her neck, tilting her face back up to him before he could stop it. She leaned into him again and his mouth captured hers.

He moved slowly, tasting the sweetness of her full lips as his hand stroked her back.

The air in the room shifted, this moment suddenly changing from an impersonal experiment to a highly personal embrace. They weren't practicing anymore. He was a man and she was a woman and they were kissing because they wanted to be kissing.

God, she felt so good.

He should pull back. He knew it clearly, like he was standing on the edge of a high cliff, considering the fall that was possible if he persisted. He lifted his mouth and rested his forehead against hers, knowing he shouldn't continue but not wanting to stop.

A knock sounded at the door and he met her eyes. She ducked under his arm to answer it, and he turned reluctantly around. A butler stood on the other side, holding up a suit and tie on a hanger. "I've brought Mr. Matteo's things for the reception, Miss Grace."

"Take them to his room, please," she said.

The butler looked from Grace to Matteo and back. "But this is his room, madam."

Jesus, I'm sharing a room with her.

He tucked his hands in his pockets. How the fuck was he going to keep his hands off her for three months? He'd only been here a day and they'd already been making out hot and heavy.

The butler cleared his throat.

Matteo walked to him and took the hanger, thanking him before shutting the door and turning to Grace. "I'm sure it's just a misunderstanding."

Her cheeks were red and she shook her head. "No, it isn't. That son of a bitch expects us to share a room." She stormed to the phone, picked it up, and dialed. "How could you?" she snapped. "This was not part of our agreement. The wedding reception is bad enough, but you expect this man to share my room with me? *Share my bed*?"

The irony struck Matteo. Wasn't that exactly what he'd just been thinking? His stare fell to the floor, unfocused. He was grateful for the interruption. He had to do better going forward, had to stay out of that situation and control his reaction to this woman.

He was a SEAL, for God's sake. Willpower shouldn't be a problem.

She hung up the phone, letting it slam into its cradle and sitting eerily still.

"What did he say?" he asked.

She didn't answer for a long moment. "That I made my bed, and I must lie in it."

The insensitivity in that response shocked him. How bad was the relationship between father and daughter if that was how he treated her? "You two don't get along very well."

"You're very observant."

Prickly. She was prickly. He pretended not to notice. "It must be hard."

"And the fact that I'm here, under my father's roof again when I never thought I'd be back—ever—is the worst kind of salt for my wounds. He hates me."

"Don't say that."

"Why else would he do the things he does? I understand the necessity of me being married. I get that. But forcing you to share a room with me? There's no reason for him to put me in that situation unless he wants to punish me."

"Grace, I won't do anything to make you uncomfortable. What just happened between us doesn't have to happen again."

Unless you want it to.

He didn't say the words that his mind was screaming for him to add.

"That was a mistake," she said, covering her face. "I'm so embarrassed."

He walked toward her. "Don't be. It's my fault. It was my idea and I got carried away."

"It felt good to forget about my problems for a second. To feel something besides awful." She shot him a sideways glance. "It's nothing personal."

They didn't even know each other. Of course it wasn't personal. So why did her comment make him want to show her just how personal it could be?

She crossed her arms over her chest. "I think it would be best if we leave each other alone as much as possible."

"I disagree. This whole situation would be easier if you and I were friends. If we could trust each other and get along well, it would go a long way toward making the next three months easier on both of us."

"You don't get it, do you? You work for him. He will

exploit that and he will use it to his advantage in any way possible. You are nothing more to him than a well-paid spy."

The idea that Vasile might treat his own daughter so horribly was appalling. Either Grace was out of her mind, wrongfully convinced of the lengths her father would go to, or the man had no sense of right and wrong where his daughter was concerned. Both of those possibilities were disturbing.

"I'm also your husband."

She laughed out loud. "You're kidding now, right?"

He took in her features, from her angry green eyes to her patrician nose and the posture that spoke of long nights with her infant son. "I know we're not really in a relationship, but we are legally married. And in the Church. I don't take that lightly. You and I may not be a traditional husband and wife, but you have my loyalty, no matter what your father may expect."

Her lips parted and her eyes seemed to be searching his for the truth. She was so beautiful, even more beautiful than he'd noticed before, and he wanted her trust. Was prepared to earn it.

"You mean that?"

"SEAL's honor."

"All right then. We'll be friends." She held out her hand and he shook it. "I need to lie down for a while," she said. "See if I can wrap my head around this mess before we get paraded around like prized cattle."

"Fine. I'll give you some space."

8

Matteo spent the next hour and a half exploring the house and getting a mental map of the premises. There were fourteen rooms downstairs and eight bedrooms upstairs, each with their own bathroom and most with their own fireplace. The third floor was a combination of storage space and what seemed to be quarters for the staff.

He'd have to get a list of everyone who worked here for Logan to research.

He checked out the security system inside the residence, from cameras and motion sensors to contact alarms on the windows and doors.

An hour in, he found what he was looking for. There, on the contact for a side entrance to the house, was a thin piece of metal.

"Bingo."

If this door was opened, the metal would make it seem like the contact was still attached. Whomever had gotten into the baby's room had most likely come in through this door.

He moved into the motion sensor hidden in a corner of the room, suspecting that it, too, had been tampered with. He opened up the back of the unit with his Swiss Army knife. Sure enough, the wires inside the motion sensor had been cut.

He made his way to Nico's room, stopping to check each piece of the security system in between. A clear path had been created from the point of entry to the crib.

Whomever was working inside the house knew exactly where the intruder was headed.

He needed to find out where the main security system was located and check out the circumstances of the missing surveillance tapes.

The security advisor had said the staff who could have been responsible for the security breach had been dismissed, but the existence of a mole meant true security was nothing but a farce.

Still, he would use those names as a starting point.

He frowned. The solitary nature of this assignment meant he must detail without his greatest weapon — the other members of HERO Force. They were a team, and a damn good one. It would be a challenge to protect Grace without them.

His mind wandered back to her phone call.

You expect this man to share my room with me? Share my bed?

He couldn't help but wonder if that was really what would happen. He could still taste her on his lips, feel the softness of her cheek beneath his fingertips. What the hell had gotten into him? He barely knew her. But she was so damn vulnerable with that hard shell and soft interior, the combination making him admire her and want to make it better at the same time.

Fuck.

He was already in up to his knees and he had to get terra firma beneath his feet before he fell right in. He forced his attention back to the task at hand. The security system needed some serious upgrades before he was confident in its ability to protect anyone. He took out his phone and called the general, explaining in detail what he wanted.

He'd just hung up when something odd caught his attention. There in the fold of the sitting room drapes was something that didn't belong. He pulled down the curtain rod and picked out a small electronic device.

A bug.

Someone had wiretapped this room.

He looked around. Out of all the rooms he'd explored so far, this one seemed no more notable than the others. If it was bugged, there was a good chance they all were. He carefully put the listening device back where he'd found it before going in search of Vasile.

He found him in his study.

"You're settled in, I assume?" asked the president.

Matteo took a seat. "I am."

The older man nodded sagely. "I'm sure you were surprised to learn where you'd be sleeping."

He seemed to be fishing, looking for a reaction, and Matteo kept his face carefully blank. "A bit."

"Thirty-two people work in this household. That number does not include my office staff, nor the many people who come in and out of this building on a regular basis. I need your marriage to my daughter to appear sincere on every level."

"I understand."

"She does not. She can be difficult, as you may have

already surmised. She was not happy she had to marry, but she does understand it is necessary."

One question was already lingering in Matteo's mind. "Then why not have her marry the baby's father?"

"I can only assume he is no longer in her life, but I'm not sure of that. She won't tell me who he is."

"I'm sure she will tell you in her own time."

"Do you have children, Mr. Cruz?"

"Matteo. No."

The older man leaned forward on his desk, holding his hands. "Lenore and Grace were inseparable."

"Lenore?"

"My wife. She passed away several years ago. While Grace and I have never been close, she now seems to hold me in contempt, as if losing her mother was somehow my fault. I daresay she would sooner die than reveal her heart to me."

The sadness in the old man's eyes touched Matteo. He hoped to have kids of his own one day and could not imagine such a bad relationship with one of his own children.

"But she might tell you," Vasile said. The stare he gave Matteo made his expectations crystal clear.

You are nothing more than a well-paid spy.

"Sir, if you had hired me to be your daughter's bodyguard, I would be liable to you. Likewise, if you hired me to be your advisor or a valet or the head of the Armed Forces, I would be liable to you. But you hired me to be your daughter's husband. My loyalty lies with Grace."

"It is not a real marriage in any way. You are no more than an actor, and I, the producer."

"I don't see it that way."

"Then I suggest you change your thinking, or I will get HERO Force on the line and clarify your responsibilities."

Matteo sat forward in his chair. "Don't you see what you're doing to her?"

"Rubbish. I don't need to listen to advice from my staff."

"She's just had a baby. She's tired and overwhelmed and stressed. You asked her to marry a stranger and she did that for you. Then you insisted she share her private space with me and you shamed her when she objected. Now you want to make sure she doesn't have a confidant in me. And you wonder why she doesn't trust you?"

Vasile stood up, his height a near-perfect match for Matteo's. "You will be replaced. I will call Mr. Wilson and tell him your services are no longer required."

"The ceremony is done. There will be no replacement. Grace is my wife." The grandfather clock on the wall struck seven. "Time for the reception, unless you'd like to go out there and explain to them why your daughter's new husband won't be attending?"

The two faced off for several moments.

The phone on Vasile's desk rang and he picked it up. "Yes?" he snapped.

The color seemed to drain from Vasile's face.

"When?" he asked, then he was quiet, listening. "Get Talia in here." He hung up the receiver and looked back at Matteo.

"They just found a bomb at a baseball game. More than five hundred people in the stands, not counting the players. They are sending the bomb squad to diffuse it." He leaned back in his chair. "This isn't the first time—"

Matteo held up his hand to stop Vasile from talking, then held a finger to his lips to warn him to be quiet. He picked up a pen from the president's desk and wrote on a small pad. THE ROOM IS BUGGED.

Vasile furrowed his brow and raised sharp eyes back to Matteo's.

"I'd like you to show me around the grounds if you have time," said Matteo.

"I suppose I can do that."

9

Cowboy was on the firing range with five potential new hires. Today he was testing their knowledge of weapons and their ability to shoot on target under stress.

His cell phone vibrated in his pocket as the recruits emptied their magazines, and his cock tingled. Charlotte had been texting him inappropriate pictures of herself for the last two hours, telling him to come home.

Her plan to move in with her brother hadn't quite worked out since Cowboy wouldn't let her out of his bed.

Talk about working under stress.

He couldn't look at that shit without getting hard, so he ignored it, taking his ear protection off when the last man turned toward him. "Nice job. For our next challenge, I want you to suit up in full body armor and head out to the outdoor range."

His cell phone vibrated again. She was insistent, and he liked it. Maybe he would go home for an extended lunch break. He licked his lips before realizing it was a phone call and checked the caller ID.

Red.

"I need to take this. Suit up and take a break until I'm through." He answered the phone. "'Bout time you checked in," he said. "I was beginning to think you ran off to Vegas with some hooker and got married. Oh, wait... That's right. You're already married."

"How's it going without me?"

"Pretty good. Running some drills with a few recruits."

"Anybody good?"

"Too early to say."

"How many women are you looking to hire?"

"At least two. But we need to bring on two or three more guys. Give us some flexibility. Like now, you're off in Lala Land for three months and we don't have a pilot. I mean, shit — Logan can technically fly a plane and Hawk can get the bird in the air, but I wouldn't get on board with either one of their asses unless the alternative was flaming lava and The Rapture."

"Yeah. We could use more redundancy. Maybe even bring on another tactical guy like Jax, now that he's spending more time out of the office."

"I was thinking about that. I'll bring it up to him. How's it going over there?"

"Different than I expected. I want you to get some information for me on the woman."

Cowboy smiled. "Your wife?"

"Cut the shit."

"Come on now," said Cowboy. "You can't expect me not to have a little fun. You looking forward to your wedding night? I should probably tell you about the birds and the bees before you turn off the lights."

"If you only knew."

Cowboy narrowed his eyes. "Red, what's going on over there?"

"Nothing, man."

Shit would get complicated pretty quick if he really got involved with that woman.

"She was in Switzerland up until recently," said Matteo. "I want to know who she was with."

Cowboy pinched the skin between his eyes. "Is she pretty?"

"What does that have to do with anything?"

"So she's beautiful." He clucked his tongue. "Be careful, Red. Don't do anything I wouldn't do."

"Speaking of which, how's Charlotte?"

The last picture she texted him flashed in his mind and his dick bounced in the shorts. "She's good. Real good."

"How's Logan handling it?"

"You mean, has he started speaking to me in the two days since you left? No. Still yes sir, no sir kind of bullshit. Between you and me, I think that boy needs to get laid. Loosen up a little."

"According to Hawk, he's quite the ladies' man."

"No freaking way."

"It's true. He said the women can't get enough of him. The older women, in particular."

Cowboy laughed. "You've got to be shitting me. Doc and the cougars?"

"I believe Hawk's words were, 'He has very sophisticated taste in women.'"

"Well, who would've thought it?" He shook his head. Oddly enough, he could picture it. Logan with his pretty-boy muscles and some knockout forty-five-year-old bombshell.

It takes all kinds.

"So Switzerland, eh? What are we looking for?"

"The father of her baby. I'm thinking it's probably the same guy."

"Roger that. Find out who your wife was banging in the Alps. Got it."

"Asshole."

Cowboy laughed. "Seriously, man, why do you want to know this shit?"

"I can't put my finger on it, but there's more going on here than just the election. I'm feeling like I'm in the dark."

Cowboy nodded. "I'll put Logan on it right now. I'll give you a call as soon as I find anything out. Is that it?"

"The whole mansion is bugged."

"Probably Trane. The guy he's running against."

"Could be. I haven't figured out who the bad guys are yet."

Red really was operating in the dark, his connection to HERO Force his only assistance, and Cowboy felt a moment's concern. "Plot twist, brother. It's you and me."

"Sometimes it feels that way, man."

Cowboy knew exactly what he meant. "Stay safe, Red. Don't trust anybody, and I'll get back to you as soon as I know something."

10

M atteo needed to stay the course. It was an expression used by his commander in BUD/S training time and time again. Don't get distracted. Ignore everything except your goal. An image of himself in Hell Week rose up in his mind, his body more fatigued than he knew was possible, his mind determined and focused.

He couldn't let the apparent simplicity of this assignment make him undisciplined. Pretend to be Grace's husband until the election, keep her safe, go back to the States and get an annulment. Period.

Keep his hands off her. His mind, too.

He brushed a piece of lint off his jacket. His suit looked expensive, with satin lapels on the jacket and French cuffs on the shirt. He'd never worn anything like it.

This assignment was chock full of surprises.

Like Grace.

He remembered their kisses, adrenaline instantly surging through his bloodstream.

Dammit.

She was intriguing, and he needed to keep his interest in check. He thought of the baby, wondering who his father was and what had become of his relationship with Grace.

Was it possible he was the one who left the note in the baby's nursery? Better question—did he even know the baby existed?

He straightened his tie. The question was a deeply personal one for him, having grown up with a single mother as his only parent. He never met his own father, and more than once as a kid, he told himself maybe his dad didn't know he existed at all.

Because then he wasn't so unwanted.

Shit.

If he lived to be a hundred and ten, he'd still act like a five-year-old where his father was concerned, and this assignment was hitting a little too close to home.

His phone rang and he pulled it from his pocket, not recognizing the number. "Cruz."

"This is General Talia. The bomb at the stadium just exploded. More than half the lives were lost."

Matteo made the sign of the cross. "*Dios mio,*" he whispered.

"It gets worse. Moments before the blast, I received a phone call from the house's outgoing line, telling me it was about to happen."

Matteo frowned. "I don't understand."

"The call came from inside the house. The bomber is here for your reception."

11

G race reached her hand inside her dress, pulling at the tight fabric. "I guess it will have to do. The others don't fit at all."

She eyed herself in the mirror with some concern. The cream-colored organza dress had two straps of gathered material that widened to cover each breast before joining her full skirt at her waist. Her back was bare.

The clothing in her closet could have belonged to a stranger, so different were her proportions and figure than they used to be. Where she had once been flat, she was now curvy; where she had once been curvy, she was now lushly endowed. She slipped a sideways glance at the maid. "Is it too much?"

The young girl's eyes widened. "Oh, no. You look ravishing."

Grace looked back at her reflection. "Ravishing?" She turned away from the mirror and opened her clutch, checking to be sure she had everything.

What should the bride bring to a fake wedding reception?

She snapped it shut.

"Is there anything else you'll be needing?" asked Trudy.

"Yes, please. Bring me the baby so I can feed him before I go."

"Of course."

Bring me the baby.

She'd only been back in her father's house a few days, and already it had changed the way she mothered her own child. The security was necessary. The space was not.

After his birth, she'd spent eleven days alone with her new son and could count on her fingers the number of times he'd been separated from her body. She nursed him, cuddled him, and slept beside him, breathing in his sweet breath and enjoying the slowing of time.

Now Nico had his own room across the hall and there were other people to tend to him. What had started as a mere convenience was now feeling like a wedge designed to separate her from her child.

Stop it. No one here is trying to distance you from your son.

Even still, she decided he would spend tonight with her, in her bed.

Will Matteo be in your bed, too?

An electric thrill ran up her spine and she quickly shook her head. No. He could sleep on the floor.

She remembered the heat that had rushed between her legs at the first touch of his lips on hers. It'd been too long since she'd been with a man. She'd been too lonely, too desperate for a man's comforting touch.

That explained her reaction.

Just the other day her obstetrician gave her the green light to have sex again, and Grace had laughed, a hysterical sort of giggle as she was struck by the difference between her life when she'd gotten pregnant and her life today. She'd gone from what she thought was a committed relationship to a veritable self-imposed cloister.

She wouldn't be having sex anytime soon.

Kissing Matteo had tapped into the well of lust that had been filling since her lover disappeared. It wasn't that she wanted that man. She was hormonal and emotionally wrecked, combustible material everywhere, and he was a match.

Yes. That must be it.

The door opened and the maid entered, quickly settling the babe in Grace's arms.

"Hi, sweetheart," she whispered to her son, all other thoughts vanishing in an instant. She would never get over her awe of this child, the weight of his sweet little body, the warmth of him against her skin. He was nuzzling her chest with his face and she smiled happily before sitting down, removing the strap of her dress, and offering him her breast.

She leaned back and began to rock.

God, it felt good to have that strap off her shoulder. With the added heft of her engorged bosom, it was digging into her uncomfortably. She sighed. It was going to be a long night, both physically and emotionally.

She took in the baby's features, letting her finger smooth over his dark brow, noting its familiar shape. It was not the only place she saw her lover in their child. Nico also had his father's full lips and long eyelashes.

She closed her eyes tightly. She would not think about him tonight. This evening was going to be hard enough without opening that particular Pandora's box.

The baby's tiny hand fisted her skin and he made a contented humming sound. She could do this forever, but she was all too aware of the crowd gathering downstairs and the maid waiting to collect her son.

There was a knock at the door and she covered herself. Would she never be able to nurse her baby in peace? "Come in."

Matteo's dark suit jacket and stark white shirt set off his complexion. He looked like a playboy or a model, too handsome to be mistaken for an ordinary man. "I'm ready to go downstairs whenever you are," he said.

"Just let me finish nursing the baby."

He walked to the other end of the room. "How often do you have to feed him?"

"Every three hours. Sometimes he goes for a longer stretch during the night."

"You must be tired."

"Yes. Very."

"I'd be happy to help if there's anything I can do. I'm not used to having nothing to do all day."

"What exactly do you do for..."

"HERO Force. All sorts of things."

"Does it stand for something?"

"Hands-on engagement and recognizance operations."

"Hands-on engagement? Like fighting?"

"When we have to, yes. Sometimes we protect people, like I'm protecting you. Other times we need to rescue someone who's been kidnapped or held hostage."

"Sounds dangerous," she said.

"It can be."

"What did you do before that?"

"I was a Navy SEAL. Most of the HERO Force guys are SEALs."

"Wow." Grace readjusted her dress as best she could, then lifted the baby to her shoulder to burp him. "And now you have nothing to do but pretend to be my husband."

"I can think of worse jobs." His smile was endearing.

She sat up straighter. "Please don't do that."

"What?"

"Flirt with me." She swallowed against the knot in her throat. "We kissed. It doesn't mean anything."

"I never thought it did."

"You were flirting with me just now." She looked around the room. "There is no one here but the two of us, so there is no reason for you to do that."

Matteo stood, looking down at her from his full height. "You don't want me to be nice to you unless we have an audience. Got it. And I shouldn't take our practice kiss or any loving looks you throw my way in public to heart."

"I don't mean to offend you. I think some men might get the wrong idea in this situation." She stood up.

"Can you take him for a minute, please? I need to finish getting ready."

He took the baby, awkwardly at first, settling him in the crook of his arm. "How old is he?"

"Six weeks."

"Your father wants me to find out who his father is."

"*What*?"

Matteo held up his hand. "But I meant what I said earlier, Grace. I told him I won't be his spy. He can't ask me to be your husband and ask me to betray you in the same breath."

The maid reappeared at the door, hovering and wringing her hands.

"What is it, Trudy?" asked Grace.

"I don't want to ruin your evening, but there was an explosion just now at the baseball field. The stadium your father had built. They're saying it was a bomb."

Grace's mouth hung open. "Was anyone hurt? Was there a game going on?"

"I don't know. My boyfriend just texted me the news. Isn't it awful? First the pedestrian bridge, now this."

Too many tragedies for one small nation. Whereas one could be an accident, a bomb most certainly was not. She turned to Matteo. "We should cancel the reception."

"The guests are already here." He handed the baby to Trudy. "I'm sure your father will say a few words. We should get downstairs."

12

They walked down the long hallway she had walked down a thousand times before. "When I was a kid, I used to imagine I was a queen walking down this hallway and that monstrous staircase at the end. Today I fully expect to topple down every last step."

"We're going to do just fine."

"We're about to pretend to be husband and wife in front of thousands of people."

"No, we are husband and wife. We only have to pretend to be in love."

He was right, of course, but she wasn't sure she knew how to do that, wasn't sure she trusted this man enough to act out the scene that was required of them.

They paused on the top step, taking in the throngs of people below, and she clutched his arm more tightly. One by one, heads turned to see the newly married couple, and Grace's stomach danced with anxiety.

Her eyes met her father's and he raised his glass. After all the years she had fought against him, all the distance she had put between them, she was right back here living in his house, completely under his thumb.

Matteo turned her toward him and cupped her jaw. "If we were really in love, I'd want to kiss you in front of all these people. Is that okay?"

Excitement trailed along her spine. He was an attractive man, no matter this was all a charade, and her heart beat faster when he looked at her like that. She nodded. His arms came around her waist and her hands rested on his chest as he tipped her chin up and lowered his head.

13

T he crowd cheered.

Somewhere in this sea of people was the enemy—a man or woman responsible for killing tens of innocent people before clapping politely at the new bride and groom.

Matteo was focused on the threat but cognizant of the need to continue with their charade. Even as her lips parted softly beneath his own, he knew Talia's men had secured the exits and were preparing to question the guests before letting anyone leave the mansion tonight.

He also knew they weren't going to find anything, which was why he had a nine millimeter pistol concealed in his jacket, a combat knife in a holster at his ankle, and he wasn't going to let Grace out of his sight.

He lifted his head and stared longingly into her eyes as he imagined a newlywed might do.

The kiss was a calculated move on his part, a visual for the people watching that would set the tone for the evening. Everyone would want to see how the new couple got on, so he was making a point to show them before they could draw their own conclusions.

He also needed to make Grace more comfortable. The anxiety coming off her was intense, and she didn't even know about the phone caller.

They walked down the stairs to the continued applause of the crowd, a smile firmly fixed on Matteo's face.

A voice from the crowd caught his attention. "Such a beautiful couple."

This was a job. An assignment, nothing more. But it was a mind fuck of an assignment and he'd only just gotten here.

The protection detail he was used to.

The relationship he was not.

Who was this woman he found himself married to? What were the circumstances that had brought her here, that had left her with a child to raise on her own?

Did she still have feelings for Nico's father?

He wanted to know, more than he should have.

Wait until you've been sleeping in her room for a few weeks, listening to her breathe.

He could already picture her cuddled on her side, imagine the warmth of her body beneath the covers and the scent of her on the air. He reminded himself he was a gentleman—a red-blooded gentleman with one hell of an imagination.

Dammit.

Just knowing they were going to be sharing close quarters for such a long period of time made Grace an important figure in his life, maybe more important than any particular woman had been in years.

He dated, but he made a conscious effort to keep it casual, even friendly. And while several of those women had longed for more from him, he had never felt the same and they'd parted ways.

The reception was a whirlwind of introductions and congratulations. From Grace's firm hold on his arm, he couldn't help but wonder if any of these people were actually her friends. They all seemed to be business acquaintances of her father's or politicians of some sort.

When they finally came upon a couple about Grace's age, Matteo was happy to see the woman throw her arms around Grace with genuine affection. She was tall with platinum-blonde hair wrapped high upon her head, wearing a revealing gold spaghetti-strapped gown.

"I couldn't believe it when I heard you were back here!" said the woman. "What happened to Switzerland?"

Grace flashed a quick look at Matteo, the brief exchange clearly telling him how hard it was for her to lie to this woman. "I met Matteo." She introduced them. "We fell in love and got married."

He took her hand, noting her cold fingers and the awkward way they curled around his. In that moment, it seemed like a miracle no one had jumped up and declared them liars, so obvious did this farce seem to him.

He looked around the room. On the contrary, everyone seemed to believe it.

Or was purely disinterested in Grace on a personal level.

The blonde was gushing her congratulations. This woman might be the one exception in the crowd, a true friend to Grace, and he noted how shocked she seemed at the news.

"I'm going to grab myself a drink," said Matteo, trying to give them the privacy Grace clearly wanted. "Can I get you ladies something?"

He crossed the room to General Talia. "I need you to

watch Grace for a few minutes. Don't her out of your sight."
He poured himself a glass of water from a pitcher. "Everything going all right?"

"Yes. We have the exits blocked, three men on the hallway outside the nursery, another on the lawn outside of it, and two more on either side of the study."

"The study?"

Talia's eyes opened just a hair too wide.

Matteo lowered his brow. "Why do you have men assigned to the study?"

"You should speak to Vasile."

"Not this bullshit again. You tell me."

Talia closed his eyes for a beat, then opened them. "They didn't just hit the nursery. The president found a note on his desk. I don't know what it said."

Dammit. No wonder he'd been feeling like he was in the dark. Vasile was deliberately withholding information from him. Abandoning the bar, he went in search of his new father-in-law, easily spotting him in the crowd.

"I need to speak to you," said Matteo.

"After the party."

"Now." Matteo led the way out of the ballroom and outside into the cool night air. He turned and faced the other man. "What did the note say? And don't pretend you don't know what I'm talking about. The note on your goddamn desk."

Vasile pursed his lips. "None of your business."

"You will tell me if you want me to help you. If you want me to help your daughter and keep your grandchild safe."

The men shared a look, a duel of wills taking place between them.

Vasile dropped his head. "It said, 'Drop out or we'll take the bastard.'"

Matteo kicked the stone knee wall that surrounded the patio. "And you didn't fucking tell me."

"It was irrelevant. I will not give in to their demands."

"And you didn't think you should mention this to the people who are concerned for your grandson's safety?"

Vasile's face was pale, a translucent kind of gray that made him look ill. "What good would that do? Would you guard him better if you knew? Would my daughter sleep better at night if she had this weight on her shoulders as I do?"

"I don't know if you were right to keep this from Grace, but you sure as hell had no right to keep it from me."

"You told me yourself, you are her husband and your loyalty lies with her."

"And you couldn't stand the idea that I might choose to tell her."

Vasile hunched forward several inches and Matteo put his hand on the other man's arm. "Are you okay?" Matteo asked.

"I'm perfectly fine." He shook off Matteo's arm. "These are terrorists. If I give in to their demands, the threats and the destruction will not stop; they will only continue. And instead of terrorizing me and my family, they will terrorize an entire nation."

"Is there anything else you're not telling me?"

Beads of sweat had broken out on Vasile's forehead. One dripped down his face like a tear. "That's it. I swear."

For the first time since he got here, Matteo believed Vasile was telling the truth. And now that he knew the intruder's motivation, they had something more to go on. "If you'd told me earlier, it would have helped HERO Force narrow down the possibilities. Hell, they might even have found out who's doing this by now."

Vasile put a hand to his chest and closed his eyes. "My opponent is clearly behind this. Victor Trane."

"All different groups are interested in the outcome of elections. They affect a lot more than the person running against you."

Vasile's eyes closed, his features pinched.

"Are you sure you're okay?" asked Matteo.

"I need to go back inside." He swayed dramatically.

Matteo caught Vasile in his arms and lowered him to sit on the rock wall. "You need help. I'll be right back."

Vasile clutched Matteo's jacket in his fist. "Pills. In my jacket."

Matteo search frantically. What would happen to Lutsia if Vasile died? Trane would take power and join forces with Russia, controlling Parliament like a dictator. This one man had the power to stop it, if he didn't die on a rock wall outside his daughter's wedding reception.

His hands closed on a small pill vial. He fished one out and put it in Vasile's mouth. He was acutely aware of the passage of time, and his eyes scanned the guests around them, but no one had noticed the president was in danger.

Vasile's face began to pink up.

"Nitroglycerin," said Matteo.

"Yes."

"How long have you been like this?"

"Not long."

"The truth."

He took a deep breath. "A year and a half."

"What do the doctors think?"

"That I am a walking dead man."

"But you're running for office."

"You know that I must."

"Does Grace know you're sick?"

He blew out air. "I couldn't stand to have her treat me like I could die at any moment. Better she eyes me with disdain than comforts me with false emotions."

Matteo knew the strain between father and daughter, and also knew what it would do to Grace if this man died before the two of them had found some peace. "You've got it all figured out," said Matteo. "Keep everybody in the dark, win a presidency you know you won't be alive for, and set your daughter up to live with regret for the rest of her life."

"I'm doing the best I can for everyone involved."

"The presidency I can understand. But Grace would be heartbroken if you two didn't make up. Just think about it." Matteo stood and held out his hand. "Think you can stand?"

"I don't need help."

"Suit yourself, but it's been my experience we all need help sometimes."

14

He took his time getting to the bar, stopping several times to make conversation with well-wishers. By the time he got back to Grace, she was standing alone, frozen like a statue.

He was immediately concerned. "Are you okay?"

She didn't respond. She didn't even look at him.

Matteo took her hand and pulled her toward a door, not knowing where it went, intent on getting her out of this room.

They entered a large library, shelves high with books.

He turned to her. "What happened?"

For a moment, Grace's face remained a mask devoid of emotion, then her mouth turned down hard at the corners. "He came back."

"Who?"

She shook her head quickly like she couldn't bring herself to say the name, and suddenly he knew.

"The baby's father," he said.

She nodded and took in a loud sobbing breath.

"Where is he?"

"He isn't here at the party. He's back in town. Lilliana told me." Her pain was so raw and so close to the surface, he couldn't help but wonder what had happened in her relationship with this man.

He longed to comfort her. He opened his arms, and to his surprise, she fell against his chest. "Shh. It's okay," he whispered, his hand gently rubbing her naked back.

"I'm so stupid," she said, pushing away from him. "I actually thought something must've happened to him. Can you believe that? I thought he'd been hurt. I stayed there for months, waiting to hear anything from him or to find out what happened. I called hospitals. I even called his family, but he was here the whole time."

She spun on her heel and started pacing. "That son of a bitch. He left me and he came back here without even saying good-bye and he went on with his life like nothing ever happened. Like we never happened."

"Did he know you were pregnant?"

"No. I was waiting for the right moment to tell him." She stopped in front of a tabletop display of glass sailboats, picked one up, and threw it against a far wall. It shattered with a loud sobbing sound.

"Nice shot."

"I thought he loved me." She picked up another boat. "I'm such an idiot. I thought we'd be a family." She hurled it through the air. This crash had a higher pitch.

Matteo wondered what that glass boat collection was worth. "It's not your fault this guy was an asshole."

"I want to hurt him." She picked up another boat, tossing it up a few inches and catching it in her hand before winding up for the pitch. "I want to slap that weasel in the face for every time I cried myself to sleep thinking he was dead." The third ship hit the far wall and burst into pieces.

Grace put her hands on her hips, her chest heaving. "Fucking shithead."

Matteo's eyes were wide.

She was magnificent, with her fancy white dress and her everyman vocabulary, not to mention one hell of a shot with a glass boat. She didn't need the sympathy he'd been feeling for her. She needed a bull's-eye and a gun.

He shook his head to clear it.

She was straightening her dress and pulling herself together. "This complicates everything. I was three months along before I realized I was pregnant. He'll know the baby isn't yours."

"Not if you say otherwise. More than one man's been surprised to learn the baby they thought was theirs was really fathered by someone else."

She shook her head. "He'll take one look in my eyes and know I'm lying."

"There are other ways to convince him."

"Like what? Kissing? Sorry, but I don't think the scene on the top of the stairs would do the trick. I feel like such a fraud, like everyone must see right through this charade."

Hadn't he just been thinking the same thing? But he suddenly knew he could do better, his anger with the father of her child making him want to up the ante, to do anything that was necessary to help her. "Trust me, Grace. When I meet your lover, that man will have no doubt in his mind who Nico really belongs to."

15

L   ogan slid an eight-by-ten photograph across the conference table to Cowboy. "Grace Vasile rented a cabin in the Swiss Alps from October of last year until September of this year. Her name was the only one on the lease, but our friends at Interpol provided us with a forwarding order that was put in by Mason Petrovich to have his mail sent there from his home in Russia."

"Nice work, Logan," said Jax. "Do we have a picture of Petrovich?"

"Not yet. I'm still trying to get one from the authorities."

"Sounds like we found Red's wife's baby daddy," said Cowboy. "Now we just need to go on Springer to get the DNA results."

"Any word from Red?" asked Jax.

Cowboy nodded. "Oh, yeah. I heard from him, all right. I think he might be banging his new wife. I mean, not yet. Probably. Probably not yet, I mean. Or maybe I'm just reading too much into the situation."

Jax cursed under his breath "At this rate, I'm going to have to hire new people every fucking six months."

"That reminds me. I hired a woman from NIS named Ashley. She's badass, don't let the frilly name fool you. And I tried to hire a dude from SEAL Team Twelve named Austin, but he doesn't want the job."

"Why not?" asked Jax.

"Apparently he's considering other offers."

Logan stood up. "I'd like to take a look at the satellite footage from the pedestrian bridge explosion. Go back in time, see if I can find our suspect when he planted the bomb."

"Do it," said Jax.

16

M atteo laid on the floor of Grace's bedroom, more tired than he would've thought possible from a simple party. It was the pretending that was exhausting, explaining to guest after guest how he'd fallen in love with his new wife, or speaking of their hopes for the future.

Talia and his men had taken more than an hour to let all the guests out of the building. Everyone had been painstakingly matched to the guest list. The exercise offered no comfort, showing only that whomever was responsible for the terrorist attack was also trusted by the president.

The door opened and Grace entered, the baby in her arms. Matteo hadn't closed the curtains, and soft moonlight lit the room as she crossed to the glider and sat down. He could see her reflection in the dresser mirror as she pulled the fabric that covered one breast completely to the side. He got a clear view of her full breast and dark nipple before she brought her son close and began to feed him.

She obviously didn't realize he could see her; his makeshift bed was in heavy shadow. She was lovely. He considered telling her he was there, but couldn't bring himself to do it.

She was naked from the waist up except for the strap and fabric that covered the opposite breast, and as he watched the baby nurse, he thought he'd never seen a woman quite as beautiful as she.

He thought of her lover. Who would leave a woman like Grace?

She leaned her head back against the chair and let it fall to the side, making him wonder if nursing felt good. The women he'd bedded liked having their nipples sucked, but he had a hard time imagining the sensations were similar.

His cock was becoming engorged and he longed to stroke it. It was enough of a violation that he was watching her, his mind beginning to take the fantasy and running with it.

She raised her head and took the baby from her breast, readjusting him at the other side before sliding the second strap off her body. Her other breast was bare, the nipple glistening with moisture in the moonlight. He made a noise down deep in his throat at the sight of her.

Grace's head turned toward him sharply.

He'd been discovered.

Good. Now she would leave and never undress in front of him like this again.

Her head slowly turned back, her gaze stopping at the mirror. She seemed to be staring straight into his eyes. Did she know he was there? Could she see him? Or did she simply feel his lust that hung heavy on the air?

He expected her to cover herself and leave the room, but she did no such thing. Letting her gaze fall from the mirror, she continued to feed her son until she lifted his sleeping body to her shoulder and gently burped him. She settled her straps back in place and stood up, crossing to the side of the room where Matteo lay.

His cock tented the blanket that covered him, but he ignored his arousal as she settled the baby on the bed and walked into the washroom. He released a breath he hadn't realized he'd been holding.

Sharing a room with Grace was going to be a lot more difficult than he had imagined.

17

M ason Petrovich looked up as the conference room door opened and his commander walked in.

"You missed a fun party. Your *lisichka* was there," said the commander.

Mason smiled from one side of his mouth. "I should hope so. It is difficult to have a wedding reception without the bride. I'm sure you gave her my best?"

"But of course. Where are the others?"

"On their way."

As if on cue, the door opened and three more men walked in, all trim and muscular like athletes.

The commander waited for everyone to sit down. "The stadium explosion went off perfectly. Thank you to Mason for making that one happen. As we expected, they determined the call that detonated the bomb came from within the mansion. Except, of course, for the inopportune marriage of the president's daughter. What do we know about the husband?"

A man with small glasses and spiked hair opened a

folder. "He's American. Arrived in town the day of the reception. He used to be employed by the U.S. Navy, SEAL Team Eighteen. Currently works for a company in Georgia called HERO Force—the Hands-on Engagement and Recognizance Operations team."

The commander chuckled. "It would seem your girlfriend favors a certain type of man. This HERO Force—they are like us?"

The other man pushed his glasses up higher on his nose. "I believe so, yes. From their website it appears they do everything from hostage negotiations to extractions. They're skilled in martial arts and weaponry."

"But they are a public corporation."

"Yes."

The man grumbled. "Not so much like us, then. Are Grace and this hero truly married?"

"It seems so. All the documents are in order. They were married in Switzerland months ago."

Mason blew out air. "Not possible. It's bullshit. A cover."

"Assuming she wasn't already seeing him while you were still there. Maybe the little rug rat isn't yours after all."

The man swore colorfully. "She was only seeing me. I got her pregnant as planned."

"But somehow she managed to salvage her reputation and keep public scrutiny away from her father. Nothing we do affects him. It's time to make the next step in our plan."

The door to the conference room flew open and a man entered, at least a full head taller than the others already in the room. "I'm sorry I'm late. I had a lead I needed to follow up on."

"It had better be good."

"Oh, it's good, all right. I found the priest who married them at the president's mansion two days ago. It took some

—*convincing*, but he admitted he'd been sworn to secrecy and paid to forge the documents with a new wing for his precious church."

"They lied."

"It gets better. According to the maid, Grace's new husband sleeps on the floor."

The man with the glasses piped up. "It isn't love at all. Vasile hired someone from this HERO Force to marry his daughter."

The commander smiled widely. "Mason, you come up with a strategy. Find the best way to use this to our advantage before the election. I want Vasile's credibility destroyed and the public to understand his daughter is nothing more than a common slut."

Mason shook his head. "It won't work. The country is in love with the first daughter and her handsome husband."

The commander crossed his arms. "It will work."

"Enough of this bullshit." Mason leaned back in his chair. "Our plan failed. Vasile married her off to escape the scrutiny, and the wedding made him more popular than ever."

The man with the glasses cleared his throat. "We still have more terrorist attacks planned. He's taking a beating for those in the news and the polls, and the subway is going to be the worst one yet."

"It may not be enough. It's too late in the game for us to be counting on that."

"What do you suggest?"

"What we planned all along."

The commander shook his head. "No. That is our last resort."

"And we are there now." Mason leaned forward, letting the front legs of his chair slam down. "He's been warned—

we told him what would happen if he didn't step down. He knew exactly what the consequence of continuing with this election would be."

He looked around at the men at the table. They were warriors, highly trained to do anything necessary to achieve their goal. But this was different. They were reluctant, and like a dog trainer wielding a choke collar, he needed to pull them along with a firm hand. "It's time to take the child."

18

G race didn't know how much more of this she could stand. Nico had been screaming for the better part of the last three hours, and her head ached from the incessant noise while her heart ached for her sweet little son.

Clearly something was wrong and she just couldn't figure out what it was, couldn't comfort him or make it all better. In that moment, she missed her mother so deeply her eyes burned with frustration.

"It's okay, sweetie," she said loudly enough to be heard over her son's cries. "Everything is all right." Except she didn't believe that. She was a horrible mother who couldn't even comfort her own son.

She tried nursing him twice, and each time he'd settled for a bit before returning to his wailing, unabated. "I don't think babies are supposed to cry like this. Tell me what I'm doing wrong?" She didn't know who she was asking and she certainly didn't expect to get a response.

"He's just fussy," said Matteo behind her.

She hadn't heard him come in the bedroom. She turned around. "This isn't fussy. This is irate."

He held out his hands to her. "Let me take a turn."

"Have you ever held a baby before?"

"Of course I have. That one time you handed him to me for a minute when I first got here."

It was hard to believe that was only a week ago. He'd moved into her life so smoothly it seemed as though he'd been here forever. She didn't even mind sharing her space with him, since he slept on the floor and seemed to have a sixth sense about when she needed to be alone.

But he'd never stepped in and helped with the baby until now. She narrowed her eyes.

"How hard can it be?" he asked.

As if to show him, she held out the screaming infant. Matteo scooped him up like it was something he did every day. He looked so comfortable, she instantly knew he was far better with children than she was.

She crossed her arms over her chest. Nothing about parenthood was easy for her. She second-guessed herself every time her interactions with her son didn't go as picture-perfect as she planned. Her eyes moved down Matteo's chest to Nico's red, teary face.

At least the baby hadn't stopped crying. That would've added insult to injury.

"Why don't you go take a break," he said. "Go for a walk or something. Nico and I are fine."

"You don't look fine. He's screaming just as much for you as he was for me."

Matteo smiled. "That's right. You don't have to do this by yourself, you know. I can help, too."

His words were like a well-placed attack on the dam that held her emotions in check, and she nearly broke down from his display of kindness. She did have to do everything by herself. For while Matteo was here for the time being, he was not going to be a permanent fixture in her life or the baby's, and she refused to allow the staff to do more for her child than they already were.

The idea of closing the bathroom door and taking a hot bath by herself for an hour was heavenly. "Are you sure you don't mind?"

"Of course not. I'm a Navy SEAL, remember? I'm not afraid of a little baby."

She nodded, grateful for his willingness to help her and secretly hoping he wouldn't be any better at handling the baby than she was.

Don't be so petty, Grace.

"Thank you," she said sincerely.

She made her way into the bathroom, closed the door and locked it, pressing her back firmly against it with a sigh. She turned the water on, the sound instantly covering up the baby's cries in the distance. She felt herself relax for the first time in hours.

No, days.

She hastily stripped the clothes from her body, desperate to immerse herself in the steaming-hot water. She loved baths. Before she'd had Nico, she took a bath nearly every day, enjoying the warm water lapping at her skin and the soothing sound of the tub filling. But now with the baby it was difficult to get away for any length of time, and the only thing worse than not getting a bath at all was having one be interrupted.

That wasn't going to happen today. Matteo would take care of the baby for as long as she needed him to. She sighed contentedly. This must be what it was like for couples who really were married with a baby. Taking turns with everything. Sharing the joys and stresses of parent-hood. What a relief that would be.

She thought of Mason and what a great father she had thought he would be. An excellent judge of character, she was not. She squeezed her eyes tightly shut. She wouldn't think about him tonight, wouldn't allow these precious moments of time to herself to be polluted by that man.

Reaching for the bubble bath—one of her favorite scents—she added a generous dose to the running water and inhaled deeply. She needed this more than she wanted to admit.

When did everything become so stressful, so hard? These politics were forcing her life into some sort of misshapen path, and she resented their intrusion even as she knew it was necessary. She had a responsibility to her countrymen to see them through this election and into the safe, sane hands of her father.

The irony that the man who could never be a good father to her was an excellent father to her country was not lost on her. He was wise and fair and dedicated where poli-tics were concerned, but judgmental, distant, and unsympa-thetic in real life.

She sank back into the bubbles, her breathing deep and regulated now that she was alone. Maybe she should tell her father how she felt, how much she missed him.

Like it would do any good.

It hadn't always been like this between them. Back when her mother was alive, she and her father had worked hard to share the best sides of themselves with each other, but without her mother's guidance keeping them together, everything had gone downhill.

The tub was nearly full, and she knew when she turned off the water she would be able to hear her baby's cries once again. Reluctantly, she turned off the water with her toes and waited for the screaming to reach her ears.

Nothing.

She frowned. Maybe Matteo had taken Nico into another room to give her some peace and quiet. Yes, that must be it. She let herself soak to her heart's content, so when she stepped out of the bathroom nearly an hour later, she was surprised and touched to see him and Nico cuddled on the bed together, sleeping.

They could have passed for father and son. Matteo's arms were around Nico, the two seemingly frozen in a snuggle. She quietly slipped in beside them, closed her eyes, and fell instantly asleep.

19

I t's amazing what a man can get used to.

Matteo had been sharing a room with Grace for a solid week now and had fallen into a routine that left his body aching for her every night.

He would go to bed before her, lying in the darkness and waiting for her to come in with the baby. She would sit in the chair on the other side of the room in varying degrees of undress, nursing the baby while he watched.

His original suspicion that she knew he was watching was now a virtual certainty. At least once every night, she would meet his stare in the mirror.

It was all he could do not to confront her, not to stroke himself as he watched her, not to step out of the shadows and reveal himself to her, all wanting and lust. His desire was getting more intense, more complex the better he knew her, and the strength of it forced him to find some release in early morning showers.

His dreams had taken on a vivid, erotic quality that always involved Grace and her glorious milky breasts. He was becoming obsessed, even as they maintained basic pleasantries during the day. But he'd made a promise not to pursue her, and if one of them was going to cross the line, it had to be her first.

Then there was the baby. What had started out as Matteo wanting to give Grace a reprieve from her screaming child had turned into something he truly enjoyed—spending time with Nico. He never would have thought a baby could be so full of personality, or that the warmth of the baby's sweet little body would feel so good against his chest.

There was a closeness that came from sharing sleeping space with Grace and the baby, from waking up to Nico's little whimpers and hearing him drinking his mother's milk. It was a type of intimacy Matteo had never experienced with a woman, and this time he couldn't run away from it.

He awoke to insistent knocking on the bedroom door.

His training had him on his feet, instantly on high alert. He went to the door. "Who is it?"

"Talia."

"What's wrong?" asked Grace.

"Nothing, honey. Go back to sleep." He stepped into the hallway and closed the door behind him. The look on Talia's face clearly spoke of trouble. "What is it?"

"A man broke into Nico's room, but we caught him."

Matteo was used to danger, not unaccustomed to a steady threat. But this was different. This was his son they were talking about.

Grace's son. Not yours.

The muscles of his arms flexed, ready to battle and defend. "Take me to him."

The general shook his head. "He's dead. He killed himself. My men brought him in alive, but they missed the suicide capsule when they patted him down."

"Thank God the baby was with us."

"Agreed. The intruder killed one of our men on the ground and made it to the room undetected. It was the guard in Nico's room who got him."

Matteo rubbed his forehead. His heart was racing. Someone had gotten inside with trained guards posted at every turn. Not just anyone could do that.

HERO Force could.

"The suicide capsule is a hallmark of Ten Komanda," said Talia. "If they are after Nico..."

The shadow team.

Fuck.

"I want twice as many men on Nico's room," said Matteo. "The same on ours. If they came for him once, they'll be back."

Talia nodded. "There's something else. I went and spoke with President Vasile before coming to you. He is not well. He tells me you are aware of his... condition?"

"Yes."

"He'd like to speak with you."

Matteo made his way down the hall to Vasile's room, quietly knocking.

"Come in."

A single light was on beside the bed. Vasile looked older and sicker than Matteo had ever seen him.

"Talia told you about Ten Komanda?"

"He did."

"They are like your HERO Force. Covert operations. The difference as I understand it is that your organization operates with some sort of moral compass. Ten Komanda does not. I've known for some time they are working for Victor Trane. The fact that they are now after my grandson..."

Vasile shook his head slowly. "They will do anything. I

am concerned for my daughter's safety, too. Her and the baby. I need you to keep them safe."

"I will. To the best of my ability."

"Even if I'm no longer here. I need your word you will protect Grace until she is completely safe from harm."

"I will."

Vasile nodded. "I have a speaking engagement a few hours away tomorrow evening. I'm not well enough to make it. I want you to take Grace there in my stead."

"Grace?"

"You don't know." Vasile smiled. "She is a charismatic speaker with a highly political mind. We share similar political views and at one time she considered running for public office, though it infuriated her to think how alike we are. I believe she'll do it, if not for me then for the people."

"We'll be more vulnerable on the road than we would be here at home."

"It's only a few hours away and it is necessary to the campaign. This is a mountain I'm willing to die on, Matteo."

"But is Grace?"

"I believe so, yes. But she can tell you her own mind."

He nodded. "I'd feel better if the baby stayed here. If we have any trouble, he would make everything more difficult."

"Fine. I will talk to her."

Matteo shook his head. "No. Let me do it."

It was Vasile's turn to focus the questioning stare on Matteo.

"She'll listen to me."

20

Matteo stared at the ceiling long after returning to bed. The room was dark, and he was just able to make out his surroundings in the dim light coming from the bathroom. He was in Grace's bed, Nico at his side, with Grace curled up on the other side of the baby.

He must've fallen asleep, because when he woke, the baby was clearly looking for his next meal. He put his arms under the infant and pushed him closer to his mother. "Grace?"

"Mmm."

"I think the baby is hungry." She reached out and pulled him close, the sound of the baby nursing filling the quiet room. A wave of protectiveness washed over him. He would do anything to keep this woman and child safe.

This was how it would be one day, when he really got married and had a child of his own. He frowned. He didn't want some other woman, some other child.

He wanted the ones he already had.

Without thinking, he laid his arm across her pillow and touched her hair.

Her eyes opened and locked with his in the darkness. He ran his nails along her scalp. Her hair was soft and he longed to thread his fingers through it as he kissed her. She moaned softly so he knew it felt good to her, the quiet hum of satisfaction.

"I want to lie next to you," he said.

"Nico needs a diaper."

"I've got it."

He sat up, grabbed a clean diaper and wipes, and settled back on the bed to change the now sleeping baby. Then he scooped up the child, cradled him against his chest, and gently settled him in the makeshift bed on the floor before returning to Grace.

She lifted up the sheets for him to join her. For all the times he'd been in bed with a woman, this one felt the most right.

He pulled her into his arms. He could tell the moment she felt his erection, but she only paused for a moment before pressing her body against his from head to toe. She was warm from sleep, the scent of her heavy on her skin.

He kissed her, gently at first, her lips soft and slightly open beneath his. This was more than just lust, more than the tightening of the tension that had been humming between them since he met her.

His arms wrapped around her waist, one hand ending up on the bare skin of her back where the hem of her nightgown had been pulled up to feed the baby. It felt right that his hands should be on her nakedness, right that they'd fitted themselves against each other like the most comfortable of lovers.

Her hands snaked up his chest and around his neck,

holding him to her. Her fingers slipped into the short hair at his nape and he deepened their kiss, a steady pulse beating in his groin as her squeezed her tightly against him.

He allowed himself the fantasy, this woman, this child, this night. His concern for her safety only magnified his feelings. His hand moved up her rib cage and cupped the softness of her breast, gently squeezing her nipple.

A small drop of liquid appeared beneath his fingers, a drop of warm milk, and he growled with the effort it took to keep from bending his head and tasting her with his hungry mouth.

She arched her back as a small sound of pleasure escaped her lips.

"Do you like that?" he asked.

"Yes."

He lifted her nightgown up to her chin, exposing the glorious breasts he'd seen but never touched. Gently he took a bud between his thumb and forefinger and lightly squeezed.

She sucked in air.

This time when a drop of milk appeared, he licked it like a cat licking cream. It was sweet on his tongue and he swore softly at this new sexual dimension. He wanted to make love to her, to hear the sounds his wife made when he thrust himself inside her.

His eyes popped open.

Wife.

The annulment he planned to receive would not be forthcoming if their relationship was consummated. If he slept with her, they'd really be married.

Forever.

At least in the eyes of the Church.

And his mother.

And hell, maybe himself.

Grace's legs spread open beneath him and his hardened cock pressed against her underwear. He could feel her damp heat through the fabric of his boxers, feel how ready she was to make love to him.

You won't be able to get an annulment.

It was everything he'd been taught since he was a little boy, and while some of the tenets of his religion had fallen by the wayside as he grew up and got older, the sanctity of marriage was not one of them.

He teetered on the edge of decision, but when he would've pulled back, Grace sucked on his bottom lip, filling him with need. The force of it controlled him, commanded he comply, and he pushed her against the bed, his hips straining against her most intimate places.

He could have been a teenager, grinding fully clothed against a woman for the first time. He was so turned on and excited, every muscle at the ready, knowing he was gone. She lifted her mouth from his, exposing her neck. He sucked lightly on her skin, loving the taste of her and the musky scent of her body.

He had to have her. He slipped his hands into her panties, grabbing her ass cheeks and squeezing her tightly against his ready erection. Then her hands were between them, frantically working the buckle of his jeans.

He'd never been so turned on, so desperate to make love to a woman as this. But the consequences of their union clamored in his brain, forcing him to face what he was about to do. He had to stop before he was inside her, all reason and justification lost to pleasure.

With the very last shred of willpower he possessed, he moved over her and stripped her of her panties, then his hands were doing what he longed to do with the rest of his body, exploring her recesses and smooth flesh, wet from wanting him as much as he wanted her. He tasted her with his tongue and her hips came off the bed.

He wanted to see her lose control. He made love to her with his mouth, his fingers slipping inside of her and stroking the sensitive area on the front of her tight channel.

"I need you inside me," she said.

He grabbed one full tit in his hand and teased her sensitive peak, sending her over the edge.

He moved beside her and held her in his arms. She reached down and stroked him, squeezing his shaft. He groaned and put his hand over hers. "Don't."

"Why not?"

"If we make love, we can't get an annulment. Isn't that what we want?"

She didn't answer, but burrowed her head in the crook of his arm.

"Grace?"

"Yes. We want an annulment."

21

Her breathing was slowly returning to normal. Her body was tingling all over despite the crush of Matteo's words on her heart.

It was stupid they hurt her feelings at all. They'd only known each other a week. What did she think would happen? That he would suddenly be desperate to commit his life to her forever?

He moved to get up.

"Stay in the bed with us," she said.

"Okay. I'll just get the baby."

He kneeled on the bed, placing Nico beside her and climbing in after him.

He was so good with her child, everything a woman could ask for in a husband. Was it her fault she was getting caught up in this charade? That she wanted it to continue?

This isn't about the baby, and you know it.

She liked Matteo enough herself to want him to stick around, and that was before he blew her mind in bed. If that was him holding back, what would it be like if they really made love?

Don't torture yourself. It's never going to happen.

She was tired and she felt sleep trying to take her, but she fought it, not wanting this night to end. She needed to savor every sensation before she forgot how good his body felt on hers, the strength of him as he flipped her over and followed her down, the hard ridge of his erection pressing into the softness between her legs.

He's right, and you know it.

None of these things were enough to base a marriage on. But life was so complicated and difficult lately, and Matteo was so damn solid and good. Not to mention, he had a body that could stop traffic. Of course a woman like her would want a man like that to stick around.

He touched her hair again and she turned her head to see him.

"Get some sleep," he said.

"I can't stop thinking."

"About what?"

Her stomach clenched. She considered lying. "You." He didn't say anything and she squeezed her eyes shut.

You just had to tell him, didn't you?

"I think about you all the time," he said, trailing his fingers down her face.

She opened her eyes. "You do?"

"Yes."

She reached up and took his hand in hers with a sigh. "Good night, Matteo."

22

L ogan was on his sixteenth hour of watching satellite footage from the pedestrian bridge in Lutsia, and his eyes were beginning to burn. Somewhere on this recording was a picture of the bomber, and he'd be damned if he was going to give up without finding it.

Jax stood over his shoulder. "Even if you find the guy, you're not going to be able to ID him from that satellite image."

"There's no telling what else I'll be able to see. A car. Anything could be a clue."

Cowboy sat down heavily at the conference table behind them. "Did you get ahold of our contact at Interpol?"

"Yes," said Logan. "He emailed me a report on Ten Komanda, a black ops organization that's one of the prime suspects in the terrorist attacks. I forwarded it to you."

"What do you think?"

"I think it's too simple. Too neat and tidy to blame it on them. Groups like that don't just decide to go after somebody. They're hired to do a job, just like we are."

"So?"

"So, Ten Komanda might be the smoking gun, but they are not the ones pulling the trigger. My guess is someone with a lot to lose. One of the political parties, maybe even a candidate or someone with their own agenda for the country."

"Good work. Let me know if you find anything on the satellite feed," said Jax.

"I don't know, Jax," said Cowboy. "I've got a bad feeling about this one. If Doc over there is right, we might have a freaking superpower trying to kill our guy over there."

Logan turned around. "Actually, Russia hasn't been considered a superpower since the late 1990s."

"Whatever," said Cowboy. "I think Red might be seriously outgunned and we should send in reinforcements."

"It's a bit of a long trip, don't you think?" asked Jax.

"All the more reason we should go now. It's too fucking far away to swoop in there at the last minute if he needs help, and if he's up against these Ten Commandments guys—"

"Ten Komanda," said Logan. "It means *shadow team* in Russian."

"—all by himself, he might get his ass kicked," finished Cowboy.

Jax nodded. "Agreed. I'll come with you."

Logan shook his head. "Your daughter's christening is this weekend."

"Shit," said Jax.

Cowboy counted on his fingers. "Just give me Hawk, Doc, and the new guy, Austin."

"I thought Austin turned you down," said Jax.

"He did. But he's about to find out how persuasive I can be."

"I'd really like to stay here and work on these recordings some more," said Logan.

"So fire up your gigantic laptop and get on the plane," said Cowboy.

"The download speeds aren't sufficient compared to how fast I can go here at headquarters."

Cowboy dropped his chin and looked at Jax from beneath his brow. "The download speeds aren't sufficient."

Jax stood up. "Get on the damn plane, Logan. We need you."

"Sir, I don't think that's a good idea."

Cowboy and Jax looked at each other, then looked at Logan.

"This could be important," Logan said.

Jax pointed at him. "Not as important as backing up your teammate when he's got his balls against the wall. Now move."

23

Matteo and Grace were driving to the speaking engagement she'd taken over for her father. It had been a beautiful day up until about an hour ago, but clouds were moving in, darkening the landscape. He'd checked the weather before they left the house, the future radar showing their destination on the edge of a winter storm.

It was expected to rain, but it wouldn't be cold enough for the icy mix or snow that was expected just to their north.

He stole a glance at Grace. "How is it to be out of the house without the baby?"

"I don't know. I have moments where I feel blissfully free and unattached, followed by this yearning sort of desperation I can't even explain. It's weird."

"You should try to enjoy yourself while we're there. You don't get to do enough for yourself these days."

She looked out her window. "I'm worried about leaving Nico with a bottle. He's not used to that."

"I'm sure he'll be okay."

She didn't respond. He was missing the mark, and he

knew it. "I know it isn't easy. I see how you two are together and I can only imagine how hard it is to be away from him."

It's going to be hard for me when it's time to go.

She turned back toward him. "Thank you."

"It will only be six or seven hours, tops. Are you all set for your speech tonight?"

"I am. I used to do this a lot during my father's last campaign. I like politics, and I know he's good for our country. My mom always encouraged me to help him. I think she wanted us to be closer."

"What about you? Is that something you want?"

"For my father and me to be closer? I stopped believing that was possible a long time ago."

Matteo decided to let that go for now.

They'd just reached the city limits when the rain turned over to sleet. Matteo frowned. If the temperature was dropping, they could be in for a hell of a time. It was too late now to turn around, so he kept his concerns to himself as they checked into the hotel Grace had insisted they book, claiming she needed a home base.

It took her an unusually long time to get ready, and they made it to the auditorium with only fifteen minutes to spare before her speech. Grace was calm despite the pressure, as if she did this sort of thing every day and could simply swing in on a rope dangling from a jet plane, give her speech to thousands of people, and swing back out again.

This was a side of Grace he hadn't seen before. The businesswoman, the politician, and he was impressed.

By the time Matteo made it to his seat near the front of the auditorium, he was downright curious to hear what she had to say. Would she be mild-mannered and polite, or would she surprise him yet again?

A couple behind him was talking.

"I don't care what the media says. He scares me."

"Clearly, he is not being upfront about his plans for the future or his relationship with Russia. I'm just not sure Vasile is the answer."

"I know. He's getting old. Did you see him on the news last week? He's not looking so good, either. I wonder if he's sick."

The man clucked his tongue. "I wish he was younger. You'd think they could come up with a better candidate who didn't have one foot in the grave to fight Trane."

"You're still going to vote for him, aren't you?"

"I'm not sure."

The lights in the theater went down, and the couple stopped talking, but their comments bounced around in Matteo's head for the next hour. He knew Vasile wasn't well —even less well than he appeared in public, since at the house he was without makeup.

Grace was more than holding her own, clearly grabbing the audience's attention while she went over her father's plans if he was elected to another term. But from where Matteo was sitting, Grace was the one who was shining.

"I can speak to my father's ideals because I share them. We all share them. We want to live in a free and independent state. We want our children to grow up knowing they are safe in a land that can defend itself from the hostile intentions hidden in an otherwise beautiful world.

"Because make no mistake, there are those with hostile intentions toward our country and if we do not actively resist the propaganda that is being fed to us as if it were truth, we will find ourselves living in a place we don't recognize with ideals we can't support.

"Victor Trane advocates for those in charge of our country to listen to the changes being suggested by Russia.

Just listen. Let me ask you a question. Do you really believe all he wants you to do is hear them out? Of course not. His loyalty lies with Russia, and if he is elected, he will give control of our country to them."

Applause erupted all around him, the crowd instantly on their feet. Grace had issued a battle cry that had resonated with every person in that room. Matteo could feel it.

"Now there's someone I could vote for," came the voice of the woman behind him.

Matteo furrowed his brow. Did Grace want to follow in her father's footsteps into politics? He let his mind wander, considering the possibility.

What do you care? You're not going to be here anyway.

That was true. Any future for Grace would not include him, and she would be a single mother—at least until she met someone she truly wanted to marry. Considering the situation with her father and the whole reason Matteo was here, he knew that would hurt her chances of succeeding in that arena.

He made his way backstage, rounding the corner of a long hallway to see Grace shaking hands with the throng of people who were clearly giving her congratulations.

She was glowing, and Matteo's breath caught in his chest. He already knew she was beautiful, but now he'd seen inside her to her intelligence, wit, and sharp mind. Grace Vasile was the whole package, and he had the uncanny feeling he was looking at someone who would become an important figure in history.

She caught sight of him and smiled, making several heads turn in his direction to see who the lucky man was.

It's her husband, of course.

Yes, no one here would find it strange that he was

looking at her with such pride and admiration. Even if they noticed the spark of attraction that grew into a steady flame as he approached, it was all completely normal for a newly married couple.

He didn't need to mask the attraction he felt for her, didn't need to tear his stare away from the high color in her perfectly sculpted cheeks.

His body tingled with wanting her. He opened his arms and kissed her on the lips. "That was fantastic, honey."

"Thank you."

The flash of a camera went off.

His hand lingered on her, dropping to the small of her back when he moved to stand beside her. The final congratulations were made hastily, and then they were alone.

She turned to face him. "Thank you for doing that."

"What?"

"Standing here and being my husband and front of those men. They are important people to my father."

I wanted to do it.

"You did a great job out there. I'm proud of you."

They fell into step beside each other and he took her hand as they went outside. Everything was blanketed in several inches of snow.

"Oh, no," said Grace, pulling her hand out of his and her cell phone from her purse. She flashed a worried glance at Matteo. "What do you think the roads are like?"

"This was supposed to miss us. I'm sure it changes over to rain not far from here."

The weather radar loaded on her screen, vibrant colors covering every part of it. She cursed under her breath. "We were supposed to miss this. It goes all the way back home. What are we going to do?"

"It's okay. We have the hotel room. We can stay overnight."

"But the baby!"

There was such panic in her voice that concern pulled at him. "Is there enough milk for him at the house?"

"Yes, but…"

"Then he'll be fine."

"You don't understand."

"You're being too hard on yourself. This isn't something you can control."

"He's never been away from me for more than a couple of hours. He's the one this is going to be difficult for."

"I know. And I understand, really, I do. But look at this." He took the phone from her hand and zoomed in on the pink area between the snow and rain. It covered most of their way back.

"That's freezing rain. The roads have to be an ice rink, especially for the sedan." He handed her back the phone, wishing he could do something that would erase the dejected look on her face. "I'm sorry. If it were just snow, I would get you back there, but we're not going to be able to make it tonight."

"Stupid ice storm."

His arms ached to hold her, comfort her. He spoke before he could think better of it. "Do you know how often I want to put my arms around you?"

She looked at him with red eyes full of tears and leaned into him. His arms came around her. He kissed the top of her head. "It will be okay. I promise you."

"I know. It just sucks."

He held her for a long time, letting her be the first to let go. When she stepped back, she wiped her eyes and sighed.

"Do you want to get some dinner?" he asked.

"Can we go back to the hotel first?"

"Sure."

Forty-five minutes later he was sitting on the hotel room bed waiting for her to finish getting ready. She'd already been in the bathroom for quite some time, and he couldn't help but wonder what she was doing in there.

She eyed him sheepishly as she walked out. "Sorry. I had to pump."

He tried to hide his surprise and must have failed miserably, because she explained, "My body keeps making milk. If I don't feed the baby for a while, it hurts, so I have to pump."

"Oh." He didn't know anything about this shit. His knowledge of female anatomy and physiology pretty much stopped at how to bring a woman to orgasm. "I didn't know that."

She skirted around him in the small room. "I was thinking, since I can't feed the baby and I still have to pump, what's to stop me from having a drink or two?"

"What's your poison?"

"I like wine. And tequila. But not together."

The wine was no surprise, but he wouldn't have taken her for a tequila girl. She was full of surprises, and the idea of spending the evening with her was more appealing than he wanted to admit, though the last thing they needed was to let go of their inhibitions around each other.

"Sounds good to me. Chinese food and a Riesling?"

Her blue eyes sparkled. "Make it champagne and you've got a deal."

Three hours later they were sitting at a table in the darkened corner of a Chinese restaurant, a half-empty bottle of champagne sitting in an ice-filled metal bucket.

"It felt good to be up there tonight," she said.

"You were amazing."

"Amazing?" She laughed. "I don't know about that. It's been a long time since I stood behind a podium."

"Yet it looks like you belong there."

She took a sip of her champagne. "You should have told me you weren't drinking. I wouldn't have ordered the whole bottle."

"I'm here to keep you safe. Besides, I wanted you to relax. You've earned it."

"Thanks."

"Do you see yourself in politics one day?"

Her eyes went wide. "Me? I guess I never really thought about it. That was always my father's thing."

"Then what was your thing?"

She laughed. "I was the one who always screwed everything up. You wouldn't even be here if it weren't for me and the noticeable absence of my baby's father."

"Tell me about him." He should've been sorry that he'd spoken the words, but he wasn't. He wanted to know. Hell, he'd wanted to know since he first set eyes on her.

She cocked her head and stared at her glass. "*Et tu*, Matteo?"

"Yes, me, too." He sensed the question caused her pain, but he couldn't stop himself from wanting the answer. "You don't have to tell me, of course."

"I already did. I thought we were in love. It sounds stupid now because I know it wasn't true, but then it was the only truth in the whole wide world." She shook her head as if to clear it. "Listen to me. I sound like a foolish young girl."

"Relationships are always changing. Just because you are not in love at the end doesn't mean you weren't in love at the beginning."

"He told me he wanted to marry me months before I got

pregnant. I had no doubt in my mind that's what would happen. We would get married, I would have the baby, and we would be a family. We'd live in Switzerland away from politics and my father and everything that was wrong in the world." She took a deep breath and exhaled. "And then he left me."

"Do you wish he'd come back?"

There it was, the question he really wanted answered, and his stomach clenched in anticipation of her response. She had already told him about her lover, but she'd left this part out.

They were alone in a strange town, stuck here for the night and sharing a bedroom. They'd already come very close to making love. Her answer had the potential to change everything between them.

The words of the priest who married them came to mind.

God works in mysterious ways to bring us the people we are meant to have in our lives.

Was he meant to have Grace in his life forever? In the short time he'd been here, he'd already come to care for her and Nico deeply.

He was falling for his wife.

She met his eyes and the tension between them sharpened to a fine point. "Sometimes," she whispered.

There you go, you asshole. You just had to ask, didn't you?

She wanted her lover back. Hell, she was probably thinking about him while he was ogling her in the mirror like some kind of peeping Tom, longing to stroke himself in the darkness and appease this desire for her that was becoming unbearable.

He was tired of jerking off in the shower. It was time for him to let go of this fantasy.

"I'm sorry, Matteo."

"No need."

"I need to use the restroom." She stood up, taking a large black bag with her, and this time he knew what she was doing. He'd have a good long while to sit here and stew over her rejection.

It's for the best, and you know it. His mind went back to the annulment he needed to get when this was all over. That woman was forbidden fruit, and he sure as hell had better remember that.

24

B*reathe, Grace.*

She rested her trembling hands on either side of the sink and closed her eyes. Her head was spinning with the first alcoholic buzz she'd had in nearly a year, she was hornier than she could remember being in her life, and that man out there was fishing for a reason to stick around.

He was sexy as hell and it was all she could do to keep from having a real honeymoon with her fake husband. Definitely not a good idea, considering he didn't want to be stuck married to her forever.

So she'd lied.

She didn't miss Nico's father. Not ever. Sure, when she'd first come home with her broken heart she had, but after she learned he'd deliberately left her?

No way in hell.

She'd barely thought of him at all in the weeks since she'd married Matteo. When he did cross her mind, it was with a flash of annoyance or deep-seated anger, certainly not attraction and definitely not love.

No, all her desire was tied up with that man in the restaurant who'd bought her champagne and started asking her serious questions.

Champagne makes girls dance and drop their pants.

She could see him lying in the dark, watching her in the mirror night after night as she left herself uncovered for his pleasure. She could feel his mouth on her private places, her body shuddering with her intense climax, wishing he would fill her with his sweet cock.

But he hadn't done it, all because he wanted his precious annulment.

You know he's right about that. This is just a job to Matteo.

A deafening boom echoed through the walls and the bathroom went dark. Confusion mixed with a primal fear. She looked around at the inky blackness, not understanding what had happened.

Before she could even move her feet, she heard his voice in the darkness. "Grace!"

"I'm here!"

They reached each other and his hand found hers. "Come with me," he yelled over the screams of people in the distance, pulling her out of the bathroom and into a thick wall of dust and smoke. There was some light here that managed to get through the heavy particles. Things crashed around them.

Matteo pulled her through the chaos toward the light. There were people everywhere, all trying to make their way out of the space at once, sharp pieces of the restaurant reaching out to scratch her, one slamming into her side, but Matteo kept pulling her, steady and strong. She could barely breathe by the time they reached open air.

Other people stood still in the street, but he pulled her through the crowd without slowing down. She wanted to ask him where he was going, but her lungs burned and all she could do was cough. Sirens wailed in the distance.

They went around a sharp corner and he stopped abruptly, pushing her backwards. "Get down!" He shoved her beside a rank dumpster and followed her down, pulling out a black handgun.

Where the hell did that come from?

"You stay here," he said. "Make yourself as small as possible and don't move."

She cowered as he stood up and a shot rang out through the street, echoing off the buildings. He returned fire, the noise so loud she covered her ears. Several more shots and he was pulling at her. She uncovered her ears.

"Stand up, now. We have to run."

Again she did as she was told, following him through the streets on her aching hip and feet that were sore from her high heeled shoes.

Finally, he rounded a building into an alleyway and stopped running. He turned to her. "Are you all right?"

"Yes."

The light from a streetlamp illuminated a dark stain on his upper sleeve and she gasped. "You're injured."

"Just a flesh wound."

"We have to get you to a hospital."

"We need to get you back to the hotel. That wasn't just a random attack, Grace. Someone was gunning for you."

"And you took the bullet."

"I told you, I'm fine." He tucked his gun inside his jacket and put his good arm around her shoulders. "It's okay now. We lost whoever was following us, and we're almost back to the hotel. Everything's going to be okay."

The started walking. "Was it a bomb?" she asked.

"Yes. There was a flash and a bang and all hell broke loose."

She swallowed against a knot in her throat. "Another terrorist attack."

"It looks that way."

She felt as if her whole soul was trembling and she was suddenly so grateful her son wasn't here.

"This is the hotel," he said. "Come on." They walked up several steps to the top of a loading dock, and he opened the door. "Service entrance."

"How did you—"

"I studied the map this morning."

They took the elevator to their floor and he again took out his gun. "Stay here while I see if anyone's been in the room."

"How can you tell?"

"I left a piece of hair on top of the door hinge."

She nodded, incapable of words.

He reached on top of the door hinge and walked back to her. "Looks good. I'm just going to double-check." He went in the room with his weapon at the ready, returning a minute later. "All clear."

She walked to the room, noticing the blisters on the backs of her heels as she moved. She hadn't even been aware of them before now. Her hip ached, and she suspected she had quite a bruise. When Matteo closed the door behind them, she'd never felt more relieved in her life.

She moved to the window and stared outside. So much had changed since the last time she stood in this very spot. Before she'd felt invincible. Now she knew she was vulnerable to attack.

"You're okay now. We're okay," he said.

"Let me see your arm."

She could see him in the glass, unbuttoning his dress shirt, then working the fabric over his wound. The lines of his abdominal muscles clearly visible in his reflection and her stomach clenched down low. He had a beautiful body, this man who'd just saved her life.

She bit her lip and turned around. A one-by-four-inch stripe of skin was missing from the outside of his left arm. She sucked in air, her mouth making a hissing sound as she moved to him, and she forced herself to examine the wound when she wanted to look away.

"You need medical attention."

"I need a bandage."

"It's more than just skin." She covered her mouth. He would have this mark on him forever, long after he'd left her life. "You need antibiotics, at the very least."

"The bandage will be fine. The front desk probably has something."

"I'll call down."

He was right. They had a small selection of first aid items that would take care of their immediate need.

"I'm going to call Trudy, too," she said. "She can have my father's doctor send along a prescription."

"I don't want to go out."

"We'll have it delivered."

He gestured to his arm. "I'm going to wash this out."

The bandages arrived and they sat on the bed as she covered his wound as best she could.

"You make a pretty good field nurse," he said. "Thanks."

"You're welcome." She covered her eyes with her hand.

"What's wrong, Grace?"

She shook her head. "People were shooting at us today. If that bullet had been just a couple of inches the other way…"

"Come here." He held out his arm and she scooted next to him on the bed.

"You could have been hurt."

"So could you."

"But you could have been hurt for me."

He stroked her hair. "That's what I signed up for. Protecting you."

She held out a hand to him, needing his touch, and he took it.

"What if something happened to you?"

"Something eventually happens to all of us. I'm good at what I do, and I want to spend my life making a difference for those who need me on their side."

She rested her head on his good shoulder. "I need you, Matteo."

This was a dance, each step choreographed to get them closer to each other, and her spine tingled with a heady mix of excitement and fear. "I need you to protect me, and I need you to touch me and make me feel safe."

His eyes were locked on hers, his stare intense.

"I want to kiss you," she said, lifting her chin and moving toward his mouth.

"Don't."

"Please..."

"I said no, Grace." The deep tenor of his voice seemed to shake the air in the room. She jerked her head back.

"Why not?"

He seemed to be holding himself rigid and taut. She wasn't crazy. She knew she wasn't. The sexual chemistry between them was searing, and he must be refusing her kisses for a different reason altogether.

"Don't you want me to kiss you?" she asked. She felt like

she was falling, hoping his answer would save her like a bungee cord pulling her back to safety.

"Hell yes." His voice was rough and gravelly. "But if we kiss, I'll need to touch your sweet, smooth skin. I'll need to touch your body—to feel it with my hands."

Her breath came quickly and her heart beat faster.

"And if I touch you," he said, "I'll need to make love to your sweet goddamn body. I won't keep myself from doing that again. It nearly killed me the last time, not to be inside you when you came."

A hot flush bloomed over her chest and up her neck to her cheeks. She could imagine him making love to her, imagine how good it would feel.

"And if we make love there won't be any annulment," he said. "I'll take a bullet for you any day of the week, but damn it, Grace, you're in love with another man."

"But—"

He stood. "I won't stay married to a woman who's in love with another man. And you shouldn't ask me to." He walked into the bathroom, closing the door between them.

25

Matteo let the steaming spray cascade over his head and shoulders. He was wired, full of adrenaline and angst, his thoughts shuttling between his desperate need to fuck his wife and their brush with death at the restaurant.

If they were being deliberately targeted, then whomever was after them likely knew where they were staying, too.

Yet the hotel room had been untouched, the telltale hair he'd put on the top of the door hinge still in place. No one had been here while they were gone.

He could relax, be less vigilant, at least for now. Tomorrow they would be back in the car, little more than a moving target for anyone who wanted to hurt them.

This sham of a marriage was going to be the death of him. His restraint could only take so much before it would tear like a tendon that was pulled too far. His cock was standing tall and rigid in the spray of water.

It was his fault for encouraging her, for taking her to dinner and giving her champagne. Hell, he'd been encouraging himself, too. He knew all too well that he wanted her and only the slightest temptation would find him caught between desire and his own morality.

He picked up the soap and unwrapped it, tossing the paper over the curtain to the floor before scrubbing his body with punishing strokes.

He wanted her in here with him, her hot, wet mouth open beneath his as he pushed her against the tile wall.

Put a thousand men in this position and nine hundred and seventy-five of them would be a hell of a lot happier than he was right now.

So kiss her.

You don't have to have sex.

Just kiss her.

His cock was throbbing and he squeezed himself tightly. He wouldn't be able to stop if she was willing, wouldn't be able to control this desperate need to be inside her if she was begging him for just that.

He pulled on his cock, imagining her beneath him, his excitement needing no more encouragement than that visual provided. He pumped once into his fisted hand, desperate for the release that could free his mind from this damned-if-you-do, damned-if-you-don't situation. But he didn't want to jerk off in the shower.

He wanted to make love to Grace.

A good, hard fucking that could erase this need for her body forever.

Yeah, like that's going to happen.

One taste of that woman and he'd only want more.

Angry with himself, he dried off and dressed in the dark before reentering the bedroom. She was in one bed, under the covers. He slipped into the other and stared at the ceiling.

He lay awake for hours, planning what he'd do now.

When they got back to the house, he would move his makeshift bed to the other side of the room so he would no longer be able to see her with the baby at night.

He'd be polite and courteous to her, but he would work to keep the conversations impersonal and avoid being alone with her whenever possible.

No more dinner dates.

No more fucking champagne.

It was the only way he was going to make it until the election without having sex with her.

Many, many times.

When sleep came, it was fitful and full of dreams of her, so that when she walked from her bed to the bathroom several times, he thought he must be dreaming.

Then he heard her whimper.

He threw the covers back and went to the bathroom door. "Are you okay?"

She cleared her throat. "I'm fine."

He walked back to his bed and sat on the edge, confused.

Was she upset about the attack in the restaurant? Sometimes he forgot regular people weren't used to this shit. Of course she would be upset.

She came back to the room and climbed into her bed.

"I know how hard it is. You experienced quite a shock tonight," he said.

"That's not the problem."

"Then what is it?"

She sighed heavily. "If you must know, I had my pump with me in my bag at the restaurant."

"Oh."

"Yeah. Oh." She rolled over in her bed.

She'd said that was painful. "Is there anything else you can do?"

"I'm not having this conversation with you."

"Why not? I'm only trying to help."

"Because you don't get to have it both ways, Matteo. You don't get to turn me down and close the door on me and make me feel like day-old bread, then turn around and be my helper again. You don't want me? Fine. Just leave me the hell alone."

"You're in pain. I hate to see you hurting."

She sighed heavily. "Oh, for goodness' sake, drop the saintly protector bullshit."

"It's not bullshit. I want to help you."

"I hate to ruin your hero complex, but unless you have a hungry infant, there's nothing you can do."

Unless he used his mouth on those luscious tits of hers. His cock leaped to life.

Oh, fuck.

Hero complex. Screw her.

That's the problem, remember?

He ran a hand through his hair. There had to be another way to help her, though the visual of his first idea was forever burned in his brain. He pulled out his phone and went to his browser. You could find anything on the Internet.

A quick search turned up a video, and he watched it with the sound turned off. This was not helping his erection go down. "I found a video on YouTube that might help."

"Let me see it."

He handed her the phone. She watched for a few minutes, then went back to the bathroom.

It seemed like she was gone forever. Finally, he knocked on the door. "Any luck?"

"Go away."

"Is it working?"

"Leave me alone."

He walked back to his bed, but instead of lying down, he began to pace. A long while later, the bathroom door opened.

She handed him his phone.

"Did it work?"

"Yes."

He smiled. "Glad I could help."

"Shut up, Matteo."

He closed his mouth and spread out on his bed. "What's the matter?" She was quiet so long, he thought she wasn't going to answer.

"I'm embarrassed."

You don't have anything to be embarrassed about."

"Not about this. About earlier. When I threw myself at you and you pushed me away."

He sat up. "Because I want you, not because I don't."

"God, please don't lie to me, Matteo."

"I'm not lying."

"Of course you are. I'm fat from the pregnancy and my boobs are swollen and leaky and sore and disgusting. I'm covered in stretch marks. I'm not exactly pinup material, so let's not pretend."

"You're beautiful."

"Right."

He moved to her bed, sitting on the edge beside her. "You're curvy in all the right places, just like a woman should be. And those swollen, leaky breasts of yours are pretty amazing. They take care of your son, and I, for one, can't stop staring at them."

"You watch me in the mirror."

"Yes. I can't stop."

"I like it when you watch me."

His gaze dropped slowly down her neck to the open bodice of her shirt and lower, taking in her full breasts and remembering every curve and shadow. "I can't stop. I have to look at you. Stare at you."

The tension in the room thickened, the rapid beat of his pulse in his ear like a drumbeat.

This was dangerous territory. He knew when they got to this room tonight that he was powerless to control his reaction to this woman, and now the beast in himself was coming unleashed, the beast that needed to possess her. There would be no substitutions for the real thing tonight.

"I need you, Grace."

Her voice was quiet. "I need you, too."

"Come here."

She moved to the bed and he pulled her down, rolling on top of her. His hand pushed her knee away from its mate, and he settled himself between her legs. This was where he belonged. It was what they both wanted.

He took her mouth in a passionate kiss and his hips ground against hers, his erection pressing against her. He braced himself above her and hovered on the brink of no return as she moaned with every shove of his hips as if he were already inside her.

His motions were more deliberate now, designed to please her body, and he listened to her breathing alternate between pants and holding her breath. He was going to make her come just like this, with his hands and the pressure of his body on hers.

She was coming apart beneath him, lifting her hips off the bed to meet his thrusts as she pushed her head back against the pillow and called out. He could feel himself climbing, too, and he thrust harder and faster against her softness.

She wrapped her legs around his hips and the sound she was making changed.

"Come for me, Gracie. Just like that."

Her mouth hung open as she cried out, the crest of her climax overtaking her. He had to be inside her now, had to feel her clenching around him, and he stripped off his pants and briefs.

But Grace had ideas of her own, and she rolled on top of him, holding his wrists above his head before letting go and making her way down his body with kisses. She wrapped her hands around his cock and took him in her mouth as a guttural cry came from deep in his chest.

Then she was sucking him, licking him with her tongue and taking him deep. He couldn't take much more of this. Her hands came around his ass and held him to her as her fingernails dug into his buttocks.

She came up for air, panting. "Come in my mouth."

That's when he realized she was doing this for him, taking the choice of sleeping together out of the equation. Then her mouth was on him again and he let himself climb higher, thrusting deeply into her hot little mouth, her eager wetness pulling at him stroke after stroke until he cried out in his release.

She lapped softly at him, her tongue caressing his shaft as aftershocks racked his body.

When she curled up at his side, it was all he could do to lift his arm around her and gently rub her back. He kissed her hair, loving the heady scent of her on the air. "Thank you."

She kissed his chest. "Thank *you*."

He drifted off to sleep.

26

Matteo stabbed an egg with his fork, the yolk running across his plate in a bright yellow pool. "I used to steal things when I was younger. My mama worked nights and I got mixed up with some kids who made bad choices, so I decided I would be cool if I made bad choices, too."

Grace took a sip of her coffee. "What kind of things did you steal?"

"Anything the older kids told me to. I stole a car when I was twelve and got caught. I didn't drive so well. I walked the straight and narrow after that. We moved to a new neighborhood, and my mama started working while I was at school so she could keep tabs on me the rest of the time."

"But they let you enlist in the military after stealing a car?"

"I had to get a waiver. I was a juvenile, but it was a felony. They could have turned me away."

"And what would you have done instead?"

He laughed. "Let's just say I was praying real hard to get

in. The Navy gave me a good life. A better life than I knew how to get on my own."

They'd ordered room service, and Matteo's antibiotics had been delivered an hour before.

"I guess we should hit the road," he said.

Grace was quiet on the drive home. She was happier than she could remember being in months, aside from the happiness she experienced around her son. But as a woman, as just herself, this was definitely the best she could remember feeling in a very long time.

She snuck a sideways glance at Matteo as he drove. How would the night they spent together affect their relationship going forward? She wasn't foolish enough to think this meant he had feelings for her. Clearly, what they had experienced was mutual physical attraction. But she liked Matteo, and it just so happened he was married to her, at least for the time being.

Don't go thinking of him like he's actually your husband.

Yes, that was dangerous indeed. He was a paid employee. It would be good for her if she remembered that.

"You're awfully quiet," said Matteo.

"So are you."

"Fair enough. I've been watching traffic to make sure we're not being followed. You're anxious to get back to the baby, I assume."

"Oh, of course." His comment reminded her of their sexual antics. She'd been so brazen. What must he think of her now? "I didn't expect any of this to happen."

"Neither did I." He was quiet for a moment. "Are you sorry?"

"No. Are you?" She'd just had another man's child. She wouldn't blame him if he was.

He reached out and took her hand. "It doesn't have to mean anything more than you want it to," he said.

She shook her head. "These last weeks have been surreal in every way." Now he was taking a step back, giving her the option of starting fresh when they got back.

Did she want to take it?

The idea left her feeling sad. For while she knew she shouldn't pursue a relationship with Matteo, she knew she would miss him if she didn't.

"I don't know what I want," she said. "I wish I could give you a more definitive answer."

"As long as you don't have any regrets, that's good enough for me."

Regrets.

This last year had left her with a few of them. She couldn't completely wish away her relationship with Mason, as he had given her Nico. But so many of her choices had strained her already rocky relationship with her father.

"Where did you go?" asked Matteo.

"I was thinking about my father. We've always had our differences, but lately it seems like that's all we have. When my mother was alive, she was the go-between, always making sure we found a way to get along, even work together. Since she passed away, we can't seem to have a decent conversation without assuming the other one has terrible intentions."

She looked down at her ring, still not used to seeing it on her finger, and twirled the gold against her skin. "She would be sad to see what things are like now. This is definitely not what she wanted for us."

"If you don't mind me saying so, it doesn't seem to be what you want, either."

"No. It's not. In a perfect world, I wish I had a father I

could talk to, who enjoyed my company and didn't think I was a walking disaster. But I can't control other people, and me wishing for it won't ever make it happen."

"What if I told you I thought he wished for the same things?"

"Are you his confidant now?"

"No, but he did share with me enough to make me realize he cares about you very much."

Her eyes stung. Her father would never tell her himself that he cared for her, and it had been many years since her mother had done it for him. "Do you really think so?"

"You should talk to him. Life is short, Grace."

"What about you? Do you get along with your parents?"

"It's just me and my mom. But yes, we do. She's only fifteen years older than me, so we have a different relationship than a lot of people do with their parents."

"What about your father?"

"I never met him."

"Just like Nico will never know his. You seem like you turned out okay."

"If that's a compliment, I'll take it."

"Do you feel like it hurt you not to have your dad in your life?"

"It's hard to miss what you don't know. It made me wonder if I could be a decent father when the time comes."

"You're wonderful with Nico."

"I like him." He laughed. "I never realized how much personality a baby can have."

"He's got personality, all right. I just hope I don't screw him up too badly."

"Life doesn't always work out the way we want it to, but if you're looking for the good in the world, it usually turns out okay."

"Do you have a girlfriend?" The question was out of her mouth and hanging in the air before she had time to stop it. It was none of her business, yet she wanted to know badly.

"Not at the moment. I don't do relationships so well. Cowboy—he's the head of HERO Force and a good friend of mine—has been having a field day with me being married. It's a running joke."

That answer did more to stir her curiosity than satisfy it. "Why don't you do relationships?"

"Never found anybody I wanted around that much." He shrugged. "I date. I go out with women, but nothing serious."

Grace thought those women might disagree. Matteo was a great guy and she could see it would be pretty easy to get attached to him.

Not that I'm getting attached.

This was different. Sure, they'd spent the night together, but that didn't make up for the fact that he was here for the paycheck, not for her.

They were two consenting adults who just happened to have some great chemistry. And if it bothered her that he didn't want to have sex with her, that was her problem.

Matteo called Cowboy as soon as he got back to the house, taking his cell phone into the backyard for privacy.

"Marriage counseling by Ramón, where we specialize in fictional spouses. How can I help you?"

Matteo couldn't help but laugh. "You're an asshole."

"You love me."

"Yeah. Listen, we've got trouble." He told Cowboy about the explosion in the restaurant and exchanging bullets with someone in the alleyway. "We think an organization called Ten Komanda might be behind the terror attacks, and could possibly even be the shooter last night."

"Logan got the lowdown on them from Interpol. They're the real deal. Responsible for some nasty shit."

"I need backup, Leo. If they're really responsible, this is more than I can handle on my own. From what I hear, they're as strong as we are."

"I know. We're already on our way. Somewhere around Reykjavik now."

Matteo's shoulders slumped with relief. "Thank God,

man. I should have called you last night. I've got a bad feeling about this one."

"We've got a chopper waiting in Moscow. Just hang tight and we'll be there soon."

"Who's flying? Hawk?"

"Yeah."

Matteo chuckled. "Godspeed, brother."

"I know. Who would have thought this is how I'd go out?" He laughed. "No, I'm not talking about you, Trevor. Mind your own damn business. Geez. Everything else okay, Red? You didn't get hurt too badly?"

"Just a flesh wound."

"Things between you and Grace still wedded and blissful?"

"Of course."

"Are you sleeping with her?"

He shook his head. "Fuckin' A, Cowboy."

"We'll talk when I get there."

"Tell Hawk not to fall out of the sky." Matteo hung up the phone.

28

Grace climbed out of the steaming shower and dried herself off. In the days since her trip with Matteo, life had seemed to settle into some sort of rhythm she enjoyed, with him helping out with the baby and her father seeming to reach to some sort of truce with her. She wrapped a towel around her head, a robe around her body, and stepped into her bedroom.

"Grace."

She jumped a mile. There, standing in the shadowed corner of her bedroom, was Mason Petrovich.

Her hand went to her chest, emotions warring for the upper hand within her. "What are you doing here?" she asked.

He started to move, the shadows sliding off of his skin as he stepped into the light. There was the strong and handsome face she remembered, the one she had fallen in love with, the one she'd expected to be dear for the rest of her life. Her head was swimming, dizziness threatening at the edges of her consciousness.

"I had to see you." His eyes roamed her face, her neck, and lower.

"But—"

His jaw hardened. "You're married."

She nodded, unable to say more. She was confused, befuddled—a hundred words canceling each other out until there were none.

"It's good to see your face," he said. "Do you know how many times I've imagined you were in front of me just so I could look at you again?"

Her memory was recovering from the shock of seeing him, bits of history dribbling into her mind like rain through a leaky roof. "You left me," she said. "You walked out the door and you never came back."

"Shh. It wasn't like that." He reached out to touch her cheek and she jerked her head back.

"Do you know what that did to me? How scared I was when I couldn't find you?"

"If I could go back to that day and make a different decision, I would in a heartbeat."

She was shaking her head, anger rising up within her. "I thought you were dead. I wandered the streets looking for you for days. I checked with hospitals. I called the morgue, for God's sake."

"I thought you would be better off without me."

"Bullshit." She pushed his chest hard with both hands.

"I know you must be angry."

"Angry?" There was a hysterical edge to her voice she could hear beyond its volume, and she wished she could make it go away, wished she could keep him from realizing how deeply he had hurt her. "I'm not angry. I'm livid. How did you get up here? You have no right to be in this room. No right to be in my life."

"We could start again. We can go back to Switzerland or somewhere else away from politics and away from your father. We can be together."

"I would sooner see you in hell than be with you again."

He moved so quickly she was unprepared for his attack. He pushed her back against the wall, pinioning her with his body.

She screamed, and his hand covered her mouth. When he spoke, his mouth was too close to her ear, his voice too deep, and she struggled to move away from him. "I remember what it was like, that first time, when I took your virginity."

She pushed against him, struggling to get free.

"Do you remember, sweetheart? Because I can't forget, you little witch."

His mouth was on her neck, wet and hurting her, the sound of him working his belt buckle free loud like the clanging of a bell.

She opened her mouth wide and bit his fingers. He pulled his hand back with a curse, and she screamed as loud as she could, "Matteo!"

His open hand slapped her across the face, the force of it slamming her skull against the wall, then his hand was back on her mouth and he was opening her robe, yanking at the fabric.

She imagined she was someplace else entirely, laughing with Matteo as they lounged on the bed, the baby between them. Mason cursed in her ear and she squeezed her eyes shut, desperate to stay in her own little world where this man couldn't hurt her anymore.

She felt his naked erection on her hip and struggled against him as he tried to lift her leg. She heard her own muffled cries and thought they were pathetic, barely a whimper against his hand, never enough to save herself.

"Get your hands off my wife."

Then Mason was gone, and her eyes flew open to watch Matteo's fist sink into Mason's face with an audible cracking of bone. She wiped at her face with a shaking hand and pulled her robe closer around her, watching punch after punch until Mason was clearly unconscious.

Maybe dead.

She hoped he was dead.

Then Matteo stood before her, his eyes intense and searching hers. "Are you okay? Did he hurt you?"

She dove into him, desperate for the safety of his arms, the warm, familiar sweetness of this man making everything better, like cold water on a burn.

His hand stroked her hair, her back, her arms. "Are you okay?"

She nodded against his chest and opened her eyes. There on the floor was the father of her child, his face red and swelling, his pants pulled down around his knees and his penis hanging awkwardly to the side.

Men in security uniforms came to the door, instantly talking too loudly for her. "Get me out of here, please," she said to Matteo, and he pulled her from the room.

29

G race sat on the edge of the guest room bed, still wrapped in her towel. All she could see was Matteo punching Mason in the face. All she could think about was how it felt when he came to her rescue, the safety of his arms.

It wasn't just that he wouldn't hurt her. It wasn't just that he'd saved the day.

She watched him from the corner of her eye as he wrung out a washcloth and brought it to her, lightly pressing it against her face. From the sting, she knew she must have an injury, but that was her first indication.

Get your hands off my wife.

It was those words, said in a heated moment of danger. Matteo hadn't been pretending, or at the very least, she hadn't wanted him to be.

She could see now, her feelings for him had been growing slowly over these last few weeks, with every shared confidence and kind gesture, with the way the baby looked at him and the way she was beginning to see him in her heart.

"Can I get you something to drink? Tea? Maybe some tequila?"

"No thanks."

She thought of him asking to be her friend, and how she told him she needed a savior. In so many ways, that was what he had become. "Thank you for coming to my rescue," she said.

"Anytime."

She resisted the urge to talk about Mason, to tell Matteo that he hadn't been like that before.

He wasn't worth the time it would take to say the words.

She shook her head to clear it and stood up. Her breasts were full and beginning to ache. "Nico's been sleeping for a long time. I fed him when we first got home, but that was hours ago."

"I'm surprised the commotion didn't wake him."

"Thank God." The last thing she needed was Mason finding out about her son. "I'm going to go check on him."

Matteo eyed her with concern. "Do you want me to come with you?"

"Thanks, but I'm feeling better. I really appreciate what you did, Matteo."

He nodded.

She walked down the hall to Nico's room, opened the door quietly, and tiptoed into the darkness. She couldn't control Matteo or her feelings for him. She certainly couldn't control his feelings for her, or lack thereof.

This would make everything all right, the sight of her son and knowing he would soon be nestled in her arms. She'd missed him so much while she was gone and their brief reunion before his nap this morning hadn't filled the void that had been left by his absence.

She peered over the edge of his crib rail with a smile on her face and froze.

The crib was empty.

30

S he looked frantically around the room, reaching for the light switch and turning it on. The window was open, a cool breeze blowing the curtains, a dresser moved out of the way, but her mind refused to acknowledge the scene.

Someone must have heard the baby crying and taken him, trying to be helpful. The maid or her father. One of the other staff. Somebody.

She walked into the hallway just as Trudy came around the corner.

"Have you seen the baby?" she heard the frantic edge in her voice, registered the concern on the maid's face in response to it.

"Isn't he down for a nap?"

"My father must have taken him. I'm sure that's it."

"No, ma'am. Your father left more than an hour ago, before the police came."

The police. The police were here because Mason had been here, right in her room. How had Mason gotten inside?

"*Matteo!*" She was running now, screaming his name and

flying back down the long hallway as fast as her feet would take her. All she could see in her mind's eye was the note that had been left in the baby's crib weeks before.

Bastard.

Matteo was in the hallway, jogging toward her. "What is it?"

"The baby! Nico's gone. Somebody took my son."

Then Matteo was on his phone barking out orders to close the gates, call in the security team, to stop anyone on the premises.

The light of her life was gone. An overwhelming dizziness swept over her and her vision got dark around the edges. She passed out before she hit the ground.

31

Matteo was pacing.

It had all been right in front of him the whole time, and he blamed himself for not putting two and two together.

Grace's lover was involved in the plot to take down her father. The whole scene this afternoon was nothing more than a distraction to keep the household occupied and the baby alone.

Alone and vulnerable.

Mason Petrovich was in custody and not talking. Hell, they probably couldn't even hold him for very long even though he was clearly involved. He wasn't the one who had kidnapped Nico.

Matteo stared at President Vasile, suspicion getting the better of him. "Did you know her boyfriend was part of Ten Komanda?"

"I told you she needed protection."

"Oh, my God. You knew."

"I wasn't certain."

Matteo hung his head in his hands. "You should have fucking told me."

"I couldn't prove it."

"You should have fucking told me! This isn't a court of law. You thought your daughter was sleeping with one of the most dangerous men on the planet, and you said nothing. You should have told me your suspicions so I could better protect your daughter and grandson."

"She cut me out of her life completely and left the country with him. By the time she came back here I wasn't willing to ask the questions that would tell me for sure, but Talia was steadfastly convinced."

"If I'd known, I would have done better," said Matteo.

"I didn't want to lose her again."

A police officer walked in the room and Matteo pounced on him. "I'd like to interrogate him."

"Under what authority? You are the victim's husband."

"There's more going on here than you understand. I need to get in that room."

"I'll take full responsibility, officer," said Vasile. "Let him do it."

Matteo walked into the interrogation room, surprised by the intense desire he had to attack this man again.

"We meet again." Petrovich took a drag of his cigarette and exhaled, the smoke filling the small room. "We have something in common, you and me, it would seem. She is very good, yes? I taught her to fuck well."

Matteo's hands twitched with the need to hurt him once more.

"I am the man who broke in your wife," Petrovich said. "Who knocked her up with my big dick, my seed growing in her belly like a parasite." He laughed. "The bastard, come to deliver our country from Vasile."

Matteo grabbed the back of the man's head and banged Petrovich's forehead on the metal table. He kept hold of his hair and spoke next to his face. "Your real name is Vladimir Petrov," he said, repeating the information Logan had sent over an hour earlier.

Now he had his attention.

"You're thirty-four years old," he continued. "You received a dishonorable discharge from the Russian army after you were caught selling munitions on the black market. You were suspected of raping two female soldiers, but they wouldn't identify you, so you walked away instead of going to prison."

"I want a lawyer."

Matteo banged Petrov's head on the table again. "I want my son back."

"Marrying the whore doesn't make him yours. You've been doing a lot of pretending, but Grace was pregnant before I left Switzerland."

"You knew."

"Of course. Did you think I was there because I loved her? I know Grace has some delusions, but you are a grown man."

"You were trying to get her pregnant."

"Most fun assignment I've ever had. It took longer than expected, however. I can't say I was displeased about that."

"Your organization is responsible for the terror attacks, too."

"We're not that different, you and me. You work for one side, and I for another. Each of us will do what is necessary to do our jobs well."

"You took an innocent child away from his mother. I would never do such a thing."

"Come now, it's really just shifting the babe from one side of the family to the other."

"The public is going to feel bad for President Vasile. Their sympathy will affect their vote."

"The public isn't going to hear anything about this. If they do, they will also learn of his duplicity in this sham of a marriage you have created. We have the priest, minus half his leg, of course. He'll admit to falsifying the date on the marriage certificate. Either way, Vasile is out of the race. Either he steps down or he is shamed into doing so."

"And what about you?"

"Mason Petrovich is being bailed out as we speak. He has done nothing illegal, though I may need a new alias, just to be safe."

"You're not going anywhere. This whole interview is on tape."

Petrov smiled. "No, it isn't. Do you think I would be so foolish?"

A knock on the mirror brought Matteo's head up sharply. He walked into the other room, where a two-way mirror revealed Petrov grinning like a Cheshire cat. A lone officer stood in the room. "The camera's not on, buddy. I just walked in here."

"What about the officers who were in here when I arrived?"

"What officers? We were all in a meeting."

32

L ogan hung on to the stabilizing bar overhead as the chopper veered left and began its descent. "For fuck's sake, Hawk, try to keep it in the air," he yelled.

Cowboy's deep voice came through Logan's headset. "Red is waiting for us on the roof. He says they've got the local police and the president's whole security team looking for the kid. So far, no ransom note or contact of any kind."

The chopper dipped and Logan closed his eyes against a wave of nausea. "Ten Komanda isn't going to be easily defeated."

"What's their background?" asked Cowboy.

"One guy came from military intelligence after a stint with Russia's elite army unit. They've got another guy who's an ex-pat from the U.S., former Secret Service."

"You've gotta be shitting me," said Hawk. "Secret Service agents don't go AWOL."

Logan nodded. "Unless they're batshit crazy. This one lost his wife to a terrorist cell."

"That would do it," said Cowboy. "Who else do they have?"

"A research analyst. Former computer programmer and cryptologist for hire."

"Kind of like you."

"That's exactly right. They're all kind of like us. But dark. Evil."

"The complete opposite of HERO Force."

"But just as strong." Cowboy pointed his finger at each man. "If they've really got the baby, and I think they do, it's going to be harder than hell to get him back alive."

Logan furrowed his brow. "I don't get it. What does a big, bad terrorist organization like that care about a little baby?"

"Who said they care? They're getting paid. That's enough for these people."

"But a baby? Who does that?"

"It's not about the baby. It's about leverage. It's about the people who love that baby."

Logan wondered if Matteo was one of those people. "There was a picture of Red and Grace on the newswire this morning. Any of you guys see it?" he asked.

"What did it look like?" asked Cowboy.

"I can't describe it. The look on their faces is just so... They look like they're in love. Is that crazy?"

Cowboy turned to Logan. "When was it taken?"

"Yesterday. She'd just given a speech at some political rally. The caption said he was supporting his new wife in her latest endeavor, but something about that picture didn't seem like they were pretending to care about each other. It looked real."

"Not so crazy," said Cowboy. He cursed colorfully. "We've got to find this kid and bring him home safety. Not just for the president and his daughter but for Red."

33

Grace was beside herself. From the moment she'd woken up from her faint, she'd been an uncomfortable mix of frantic energy and desperation, needing to find her son and having no idea where to begin.

She was pacing the house, the grounds, going from one group of policemen to another, hoping to hear of a plan or something she could do to help in the search and repeatedly coming up empty.

Her hand trailed along the paneled wall of the hallway that led to her father's room. His deep, booming voice could be heard before she reached the doorway.

"They have no need to issue demands. The threat has already been made. Drop out of the race or Nico will be killed."

"If he's still alive," came Matteo's voice.

She stormed into the room. "Don't say that! My baby is alive. He's going to come back to me."

Matteo stood and put his arms on her shoulders. "I'm sorry. I didn't know you were there."

"At least give my son the courtesy of assuming he's alive and in need of rescuing before you simply write him off forever."

"I'm not writing anyone off," he said. "I believe he's alive, and I will do everything in my power to get him back to you."

"That responsibility is mine," said Vasile. "I've had my secretary call a press conference for one o'clock, where I will officially drop out of the run for president."

"But Father—"

"It's the only thing they want. The only thing that can bring my grandson home to his mother. And to me." Her father's voice cracked, the most emotion she'd seen him express in years.

"What happens to the country when Trane wins the presidency?" she asked.

"We pray for them. Our family has made enough sacrifices in the name of patriotism. Now it's time to protect our own."

Grace nodded, her face crumpling into tears. Her father was giving up his ideals, everything he'd worked so hard for. She knew how much that meant to him, the price he was being asked to pay. "How can we be sure they'll bring him back?"

Matteo walked to her and opened his arms. She fell into them. "We can only hope," he said. "HERO Force is on their way in. They'll be here within the hour. Together we'll do everything we can to bring Nico home."

"I want to help. I need to do something."

A knock on the door and it opened, Talia standing there. "Sir, they're ready for you now."

Vasile nodded solemnly and led the way out of the

room, Matteo and Grace following him, taking their seats to the side of the press corps. "This is a sad day for history," she whispered as her father took to the podium, cameras flashing and recording.

"Ladies and gentlemen, fellow countrymen," he began. "It is with great sorrow that I tell you I am resigning from this campaign." A collective exclamation buzzed through the room. "I will not be running for the presidency in this term or any other. I have enjoyed my time leading Lutsia, but it is time for me to step aside."

The camera flashes went crazy as reporters vied to have their questions answered. "Mr. President, can you tell us what's prompted this sudden change of direction?"

"I have decided to put the needs of my family before those of my countrymen. I sincerely hope the hardworking people of Lutsia understand."

"Mr. President, who will be left to lead the charge against Victor Trane in the coming election? Has your party nominated another candidate?"

"It's too early to say who my party will delegate to run in the election. We have not yet made any plans for my replacement."

Grace whispered in Matteo's ear, "He's leaning forward. Is he okay? Why's he doing that?"

"And he's white as a sheet." He took her hand. "Come on. Let's go."

"What's happening?"

Before he could answer her, Vasile fell to one side, just barely catching himself on the podium. The room filled with concerned noises as Grace and Matteo made their way to the front.

Vasile fell over, landing on the floor with a heavy thud.

"Daddy!" Grace screamed.

"Back up! Give him some space," said Matteo. "Get a medic in here, now." Matteo searched Vasile's pockets frantically, desperate to find the vile that could save his father-in-law's life.

"What's happening?" asked Grace. "What are you looking for?"

"Nitroglycerin."

She didn't speak again. He found the pills, quickly opening them and placing one beneath the president's tongue. He looked different this time than he had during the other attack Matteo had witnessed, his color paler, his features still.

Matteo feared he was dead. "Is there an AED in the building?"

"What?" asked Grace.

"A defibrillator to shock his heart."

One of the reporters called out, "In the cafeteria."

"Quick, run and grab it," said Matteo.

"Mr. Cruz, were you aware your father-in-law had a heart condition?"

Matteo's head snapped up. "You should go. Get out of here. We need to make room for the medics."

The reporters didn't budge.

Matteo stood and pushed at cameras and microphones. "Get out of here, now. His life depends on it, you fools. Back up, dammit." He was pushing at the reporters now, aware of the lights in his face and the footage that was recording.

None of that mattered now. All that mattered was that Vasile survived. Grace had already lost her child. He couldn't stand for her to lose anyone else.

He had to get out there himself, had to try to find Nico.

He pushed the last reporter out the door and closed it tightly behind him. His eyes found General Talia's. "I need access to weapons. Lots of them. And transportation. HERO Force is landing in fifteen minutes and I'm going to find my son."

34

M atteo stood back as the chopper landed on the helipad. Hawk was only off by a few feet. Not bad for somebody with as few flight hours as he had.

Bending at the waist, he jogged to the door, opening it for his teammates. It felt like more time had passed than a few weeks, like these men were from a different lifetime, and it struck him that he felt torn between his life here at the mansion and his former identity as a member of this elite team.

He was the husband of President Vasile's daughter, father of Nico, lover of Grace. But this was who he was, too.

Cowboy hopped down to the ground, nodding in acknowledgment over the roar of the slowing rotors. Next came Logan and a lanky man Matteo didn't recognize, followed by Hawk.

When the noise died down, Cowboy said, "Red, this is Austin. The latest addition to the team."

Matteo eyed the other man and shook his hand. "When did you start?"

"Twenty minutes before we took off."

"Welcome aboard," said Matteo. "We're going to need all the help we can get."

The men made their way across the roof to the entrance of the mansion stairwell. Matteo briefed them as he walked, his voice echoing off the cinderblock. "The baby was taken from his room this morning. We're operating under the assumption that it's the same people who left a threatening note in his crib and the president's study before I arrived, a group called Ten Komanda."

"Have they made any demands?" asked Hawk.

"They asked Vasile to resign, which he has done. There's been no further contact. We have search dogs on the way. Do you have anything for me?"

Logan piped up. "I did have some luck with the household employee list you gave me. Trudy Winslow, a maid, has been living with Vladimir Petrov, one of the Ten Komanda members, for about six months now."

Matteo stopped short. "That's the father of Grace's baby and her personal maid, who has access to Nico on a daily basis. She didn't come in today. Do you have an address?"

"Twenty-seven eighteen Wilshire Boulevard, apartment three."

"Then we start with Trudy."

The men piled into Vasile's private car, giving the address to the driver.

"Drive like your life depends on it," said Matteo.

They made the trip across town in record time, but it was still too late for poor Trudy. Cowboy broke down the door of the apartment and found her dead and wide-eyed, staring in the ceiling from a pool of her own blood.

Matteo cursed under his breath. "Quickly. Search the apartment."

The men spread out and started to move. "What are we looking for?" asked Cowboy.

"I don't know. Locations. Events. Anything that might have to do with the baby or their plan to sully Vasile's name."

"Baseball tickets," said Cowboy.

"What?" asked Matteo, coming up short.

Cowboy fanned out a dozen ticket stubs. "I've got ten bucks says these are the tickets they used to get into the stadium and plant the bomb."

Suddenly, Matteo knew what they were looking for. "The subway. Look for anything that happens to do with the subway. I think they're planning their last and final terrorist attack on the subway."

Matteo went through drawers, throwing things out of his way as he searched. Inch by inch they frantically searched the tiny apartment for anything that could lead them to Nico.

"South Street Station," called Austin from the bedroom. "Over here! I found a map of South Street Station."

"South Street Station?" asked Logan. "Oh, no. Holy fuck. What's today's date?"

Matteo looked at his watch. "The sixteenth."

Logan put his hands on his head. "The vigil is tonight. The vigil for the people who died in the pedestrian bridge bombing."

"What's the connection?" asked Cowboy.

"I watched hours and hours of the satellite feed from the bridge area. It starts at South Street Station."

"Shit!" yelled Matteo. "They're going to do it again, in the same place with the people at the vigil."

"And the subway. It's all right there, Red," said Logan.

"What time does the vigil start?"

"Nine o'clock."

Matteo looked back at his watch. "It's eight twenty-five. Move! Let's go now."

35

G race walked into her father's bedroom. She hadn't been in here since the night her mother died, something which would have made her emotional to begin with. The fact that her father was now lying on the bed right where her mother had passed away, and that he looked nearly dead himself, was her undoing. Tears spilled from her eyes onto her cheeks and she wiped them away with the backs of her hands.

When did he get so old? In her mind, he was as formidable now as he had been her whole life, but reality struck her in stark contrast. The old man on the bed was not formidable in any way.

He was frail.

He was sick.

He was dying.

She made her way to the edge of the bed. He couldn't die yet. They had too much unsettled between them, too much to fix in the time they had left, and the possibility that her relationship with her father would never be mended struck Grace in the face.

I should have tried harder to get along with him. He just wanted me to do a good job, do the right thing, be a good person. She wiped at her runny nose. Her father opened his eyes. They were gray and watery and for a minute he didn't seem to realize she was there.

"Hi, Daddy." Her voice cracked and she wished she could stifle these emotions, hide from him just how upset she really was, but that thought only had her crying harder.

"Gracie." He reached for her hand, his grip surprisingly strong.

"Why didn't you tell me?" she asked. It was the question that had been haunting her since she'd spoken with her father's physician. Her father knew he was ill. He'd known for some time.

"It wasn't important."

"It was important to me. There's so much I need to say to you, and now we don't have much time."

"I'm sorry, honey. For what I said about Nico."

Your bastard child.

His eyes drifted closed. "He's beautiful, my grandson."

Those simple words were the only balm her soul needed, and they washed over her like the highest praise. "I'm sorry I didn't listen to you more, and that I haven't been so nice to you since Mom passed away."

"I understood. She was your favorite."

Now Grace was the one hanging on tightly. "No, Daddy. You were. I loved Mom so much, but she was easy to love. I always wanted to be like you."

She watched as tears spilled from his eyes and rolled back into the pillow. She'd never seen him cry, not even when her mother died.

"I know what you're thinking," he said. "I cried for her

every night. Just because you didn't see me doesn't mean I didn't love her."

"I know you did." Grace looked at their joined hands and it struck her how time had flown by, taking hers from that of a little girl to a grown woman, and her father's from a young man to an old one. Each of them had a limited amount of time on this earth to do with what they wanted. Every moment counted.

She was grateful her parents had loved each other. Had each other to share this life with.

Just like I love Matteo.

She covered her mouth with her hand. Hadn't she known it for quite some time now? Since the first night she'd let him sleep in her bed on the other side of the baby?

They made a little family, and for too long, she'd told herself it was the fantasy she was falling in love with, not the man. But it wasn't true, she could see that now. It was the other way around. She'd been falling in love with the man and the fantasy they'd created. That perfect little family was real if she would let it be.

She just needed her son back and she would have everything she'd ever wanted.

"I need you to do something for me," said her father. "For all of us."

"All of us?" There had only been the two of them for so long.

"I want you to run for the presidency in my place."

She shook her head frantically. "You're going to be okay. You're going to pull through this."

"Even if that were true, I collapsed on television in front of the nation. I can hide this no longer. It was never my intention to lie. I just had to make sure the bad guy didn't win. I did what I did to protect this country."

"I know you did."

"But now I can't do it any longer. It's up to you." He looked at her pointedly.

"I'm not a politician. I don't have the experience—"

"The people love you, perhaps even more than me. You are well versed in the topics required of the presidency, pruned for this since you were a little girl discussing politics over breakfast. You have watched me do this job, helped me do this job, and you are ready to do it yourself now."

He believed in her.

Even more so than him asking to her to take over the run for the presidency, the fact that he believed in her—thought she was capable—was what filled her with awe. How had she ever believed this man didn't love her?

She could do it. She knew she could. When it came to politics, she and her father were of the same mind. She knew just what he wanted for the country, because she wanted it, too. And she realized he was right.

She could do this.

"I'll need your help to guide me," she said. "I don't want you giving up the fight, thinking I'll take care of it, do you understand?"

"It isn't up to me, Gracie."

"Of course it is. Just tell God that Nico needs his grandfather." She wiped at her tears. "And I need you, too."

Her father squeezed her hand.

"God willing, Nico will come back to you. But you have a larger family than you realize of people who depend on you. Of those to whom much is given, much is expected, and you have been given a great deal."

She nodded. "I know."

"You've already made great sacrifices. There will be more."

"I know."

"You did a good thing marrying the HERO man. Do you love him?"

"How did you know?"

"I knew he was meant for you when he told me he would not be my spy, that he was your husband first. From then on, it's just been a matter of time." He patted her hand. "Now you should let your father rest and go tell your husband you wish to marry him for real."

"What if he doesn't feel the same way?"

"Of course he does. And tell him I'd like to see the ceremony, so he better hurry it up."

"I need Nico here with me first."

"Then go out there and find your boy."

36

L ogan tapped his cell phone. "GPS says we're eighteen minutes away from the station."

Cowboy banged on the glass that separated them from Vasile's driver. "Go fucking faster." The car sped up considerably.

"What's the plan?" asked Cowboy.

Matteo held up his hand, his cell phone to his ear. "Talia, it's Matteo. Ten Komanda is going to blow up South Street Station during the vigil tonight. I'm on my way there with HERO Force. I need you to get word to the police that we'll be there with weapons, so they don't think we're the terrorists. And I can't get Grace on the phone. Let her know what's going on and I'll call when I can." He hung up the phone and met Cowboy's stare. "Voice mail."

"You love this woman?"

He saw Logan and Hawk staring from his peripheral vision. "Yeah."

"Really love her?" asked Hawk.

Matteo turned to face him. "I'm going to marry her."

"I think you already did," said Cowboy.

"For real, this time."

"This map doesn't make any sense," said Austin. "According to this, three subway lines converge at South Street Station, but only one set of tracks is shown."

"Maybe it's an old map. I looked it up online and they made some changes to it fifteen or sixteen years ago." said Logan. "Let me see."

"All right, kids," said Hawk. "We've got your standard issue AK-47s, we've got some spiffy new nine mils, we've got some CS gas and masks if we need 'em and some military-issue pepper spray coming at you." He started passing weapons to the men.

"Let me see if I've got this right," said Matteo. "They're going to have explosives and we've got pepper spray?"

"And righteousness," said Hawk. "Don't forget righteousness."

Matteo shook his head. "I don't think that's going to cut it. The crowd is their greatest weapon—the threat of casualties. We need a way to get the crowd to disperse so their explosives can't hurt anyone. How are guns going to help us do that?"

Hawk snapped his fingers. "Great minds think alike." He reached into a big canvas duffel bag and withdrew a bullhorn. "I figure I tell them what's about to go down, and they won't be able to run away fast enough."

"If that doesn't work, we can just start shooting. That should make 'em run," said Austin.

"Some will run, some will get down on the ground. Not what we're going for," said Cowboy.

Matteo's mind was whirling. "Tell me they won't bring Nico here. Tell me they're two separate plans that have nothing to do with each other."

The men just looked at him.

"Fuck." Matteo shook his head. "The crowd isn't their biggest weapon. Grace's baby is."

Logan turned the map upside down. "Austin's right. This map is fucked up."

The car pulled into the parking lot of the subway station, which was already full. Hundreds of people filled the adjacent park.

"The station itself is directly underneath that park," said Logan. "With entrances to the subway on either corner. The vigil is about to start in the grand gazebo, right smack in the middle of the park, and dead center over ground zero. As for the tracks, I just don't know."

"Objective number one is to clear that park of people," said Matteo. "Then we find the boy."

"Hopefully Talia got your message in time to let the local beat know we're the good guys," said Hawk.

"One way to find out." Matteo hopped out of the car and headed for a mounted policeman, then jogged back. "We're good. They've been told."

The men got out of the vehicle, immediately drawing attention with their camouflage uniforms and large black guns. Hawk pulled out the bullhorn. "Attention, ladies and gentlemen. We have a public safety situation at hand and we need clear the park immediately. The candlelight vigil will need to be rescheduled."

Everyone was looking at Hawk, but no one moved to leave. Hawk looked to Cowboy, who shrugged, the put the bullhorn back to his mouth. "Terrorists are going to blow up the subway station! Get out of here, now!"

The people ran.

"That definitely worked better," said Cowboy.

Matteo led the way. "Let's get down to the station." He checked his watch. We have less than eight minutes until the vigil was supposed to start." They split up, one man going down each set of stairs so they covered all the entrances. Foul, hot air blew up from the station as Matteo made his way down.

He could hear Hawk on his bullhorn spreading panic and sending tons of people up the stairway past Matteo. By the time he got all the way to the bottom, the only people there were the HERO Force men themselves.

The station was empty.

Matteo spun in a circle. All that was down here were some bathrooms, an empty ticket booth and the tracks themselves, the tunnels leading away from the platforms. "Three subway lines. Four tunnels here that branch into six tunnels away from the station," he said.

"And only four of us," said Logan.

"Where do these tunnels go?" asked Matteo. "What's most likely?"

Logan pointed to one set of tracks. "It's a crapshoot, Red. I can't tell."

"Fuck." Matteo shook his head. "So, we've got an eighty-three percent chance of picking the right line, and a hundred percent chance of having one of us against a handful of them."

"That's right," said Logan.

"Are the trains running?" asked Hawk.

"Who the fuck knows." Matteo moved to Logan. "Did you bring the map?"

Logan pulled it out of his pocket and handed it to Matteo, who spread it out on the ground. He lined up the drawing of the subway platform with the single line in the map, then stood up and pointed. "I say we go that way. Two go left and two go right."

"What if they're on the other line?" asked Logan.

"They're not. This map means something to them. It doesn't need to mean anything to us. They had it for a reason. We take this track." He folded up the map and tucked it in his own pocket. "Doc, you're with me. Hawk, Austin, and Cowboy, you go that way."

They started walking down the middle of the tracks in the opposite direction from the other men, flashlights blazing.

"Watch out for the third rail," said Logan. "If a train comes, we need to get up on that walkway on your side."

"Got it."

"There still won't be a lot of room, but if we flatten our bodies—"

"Logan, shut up."

They walked in silence for a hundred yards, the beating of Matteo's heart in his ears the only sound he could hear. He stopped walking and turned to Logan. "We've got this all wrong. Think this through with me. They're not going to walk along the tracks like we are. They're going to blow up the station. They've already been here."

"Most likely, yes. They would have set the charges hours, days, or even weeks before now."

"So why even be here?"

"Because they can't leave a baby in the middle of the park alone. If they're really going to try to kill Nico, they want the world to see it."

"Without the world seeing them." Matteo shined his flashlight along the sides of the tunnel. "What's so special about this tunnel that would allow them to do that?"

Logan jerked his head back. "I know what it is. This tunnel was built before the other two, before the technology to burrow so far underground without destabilizing the earth was perfected." He moved to the wall, shining his own light on it. "This tunnel isn't a tunnel at all. This was built on ground level and covered over with steel and concrete."

"What does it mean, Logan? What are they going to do?"

The other man turned toward him, his lips parted and his eyes far away. "If I were a madman who wanted everyone to see what I was about to do? I'd blow up the park with enough of a bang to clear the roof off the tracks. Send the park flying."

"Leaving only the tracks below."

"They'd be ruined. Any train that tried to ride those tracks would derail." Logan shook his head. "It would take a hell of a lot of explosives to send the park flying. More than you could hide in a subway station."

"Then how would they get them here?" asked Matteo.

A hot breeze blew down the tunnel toward them, followed by the squeal of metal on metal and the gleam of a train's headlight. Logan hopped up on the maintenance walkway and Matteo followed him, flattening himself against the wall. The train passed by like a moving picture, loud and rumbling.

They hopped back down onto the tracks and looked at each other with complete understanding.

"Run!" they both yelled.

37

Grace rode with Talia to the park, anxiety making her palms sweat and her head pound. They pulled into a train station parking lot.

"This is the wrong station," she said. "You said South Street Station. This is Wall Street Station."

"The next closest one. It will be safer for you to get out here. Come now, we must hurry."

She followed him down the steps to the station below. A train sat waiting.

"Get on the train," he said.

"What? No. Where is Matteo?"

Talia pulled a gun out of his jacket. "Get on the train if you ever want to see your baby again."

She held her breath, suddenly shaking. "Please. Tell me where he is. I'll give you anything you want."

"I want you to get on that goddamn train!"

She turned and got on. Talia stood in the doorway, the weapon trained on her.

"Where is Nico?"

He ignored her.

"I'll give you safe passage out of the country. Money. Anything."

Talia laughed. "I don't want anything from you."

A loud boom resonated through the underground tunnel and she put a hand on either side of her seat, bracing herself against the vibrations. "What was that?"

"That, my dear, is my cue." He stepped back and the door to the subway car closed.

She shot out of her seat and banged on the glass. "Wait! What's going on? What's happening?" She continued to bang on the glass as the car kept moving.

The train pulled out of the station, leaving Talia behind and Grace's train car hurtling forward. She ran car by car to the engine. There had to be a conductor, someone who could let her off this thing, but when she reached the front car, she found it completely empty.

She was alone.

A light up ahead on the tracks, and she squinted to make it out. What was so bright? It almost looked like... daylight.

Her eyes widened as her mind made sense out of what she was seeing. The tunnel was open to the outdoors, the tracks blocked and obstructed.

38

C owboy shined his light back toward South Street Station. "That was a bomb. A big fucking bomb."

They'd heard the train coming, felt the wind as it moved down the tunnel, then the explosion. They were only a quarter mile or so out of the station when it happened and it felt like the earth was splitting in two.

"That was more than a few blocks of C4," said Austin.

"You're right," said Cowboy. "More like a train full of dynamite."

"So that's it, then," said Hawk. "Bomb detonated, party over."

Cowboy scratched his head. "I guess so, but we're not going to get out that way, so let's keep walking to the next station. I hope Grace's kid is okay."

Hawk stopped walking. "Wait. Do you feel that?"

Wind, coming toward them. "There's a train coming this way."

"It's going to run right into the rubble at South Street Station."

"Fuck. How do we stop a train?" asked Cowboy.

"The third rail gives it electricity," said Austin. "You have to find some way to short it out."

"That giant fucking explosion didn't short it out?" yelled Cowboy.

"It couldn't have, or the train wouldn't be moving. Quick. We look around for metal. If we can connect the third rail to the running rail, the electricity will stop," said Austin. "But we have to hurry."

Cowboy shined his flashlight up and down the sides of the tunnel. "There! On the next track. There are pieces of metal." He ran over there and tried to pick one up. It didn't budge.

The wind was getting stronger.

The other men each grabbed on. "Lift on one, two, three," said Austin. Together they were able to just get it off the ground. "We need to drop it on the track on my count. As soon as you let go, get the fuck out of the way." The train's metal wheels squealed on the bend in the track, the rumble of the locomotive getting louder. "Ready? Just a few more feet. Good. On three. One, two, three!"

The men dropped the steel onto the tracks and scattered in the opposite direction, pressing their bodies against the side of the tunnel. Sparks flew as the train rounded the bend, then everything went dark, including the lights on the train. Its engine was quiet.

"Woot!" yelled Cowboy. "We did it!" They'd stopped the train from crashing into the debris. It was only in the silence that followed their congratulations that he heard the cries of a baby coming from inside.

39

G race was curled into a ball beneath the covers, her body like a shield around her son. Their train cars were perfectly coordinated to crash into the rubble at the South Street Station at the same time.

Both were saved by the men of HERO Force.

Matteo watched them sleeping with a heavy, grateful heart.

He moved to the bed and climbed in beside her, opening his arms for her and the baby to cuddle against his side.

"I thought you were sleeping," he said, kissing the top of her head.

"I thought I lost you both," she whispered.

He could feel her tears, wet on her face and dripping onto his chest. Every emotion he had held in check throughout this day gathered in his throat, constricting his airway and choking his ability to keep it in check any longer.

He squeezed his eyes tightly shut, tears escaping at the corners, and pulled her more against his side. She was fitted tightly against him, her leg tucked over his leg, her arm around his waist, and he knew he'd never held another woman with such intensity of emotion before in his life.

"I want to make love to you, Grace."

"What about the annulment?"

"I don't want it." He touched her face. "I want you."

It was as natural as dusk following sunset, and he knew there would be no more considering. He needed to be with her just as much as she needed to be with him.

She was his wife.

He turned toward her and kissed the top of her head, then her head turned up to his and he kissed her on the mouth. This was when the marriage would become real, and every move of his hands and his body showed her how much he loved her.

40

Matteo reclined on his side, baby Nico babbling on the bed next to him. He touched the baby's feet, with his super-soft skin, pudgy rounded tops, and tiny perfect toenails.

His eyes went to the TV on the dresser. Grace looked beautiful in a bright blue suit, the flag waving behind her in the sunshine as she announced her candidacy for president.

"That's your mama," he said to the baby. "She's going to be in charge of the whole country. You should be very proud of her."

Nico babbled his agreement.

"I'm proud of her, too." He truly was. These last three months he'd seen her go from a woman who was unsure of herself and looking for approval to someone who could stand up and lead as she clearly was meant to all along. As his father-in-law predicted, the people loved her even more than her predecessor, and Lutsia's future looked promising and great.

He turned back to the baby, rubbing his belly, making him laugh.

Grace entered the room, a wide smile on her face as she began unbuttoning her jacket. "How'd I do?"

Matteo stood up and wrapped his arms around her waist. "You were amazing."

The baby grabbed his feet, his noises now higher and happier still. He showed no ill effects from his ordeal, quickly slipping back into his routine with his mother and Matteo.

A knock at the door and Vasile walked in, smiling and scooping up his grandson. "There's my little man." Before the door could close behind him, Cowboy and Hawk walked in.

"You about ready to go?" asked Cowboy.

"Yeah. I am. Just let me get my things."

He stood up, his stare set on Grace. "Guess I'll be seeing you around."

"I guess so."

He walked out of the room with the men of HERO Force by his side. It could be no other way.

"I still think I should have been your best man," said Cowboy.

"You are. You both are."

"Hawk doesn't love you the way I do, Red."

Matteo put his arm around Cowboy. "I'm going to miss you guys."

An hour later, he was standing beneath a white arbor in the sand, staring at Grace as they renewed their vows.

"When you first came to this country," she said, "I thought you were only interested in the money. That I was just another job to you. But then I got to know you, and spend time with you, and then I got to like you. And I realized you didn't take this job for the money at all, that you did it to help the people of Lutsia, because that's just the kind of man you are." She took a breath, her bottom lip trembling. "And then I realized I loved you."

"I promise to take care of you, Grace. As much as any world leader needs taking care of. I promise to be a good father to Nico and to any more children we have along the way. You're the only person I ever wanted to spend my life with."

The priest leaned heavily on a cane, but his smile was wide and true. "Aren't you glad we didn't skip the vows that time?" he asked. "By the power invested in me by the holy Church and the People's Republic of Lutsia, I now pronounce you husband and wife."

41

C owboy sat at his desk staring into space as he listened to the hubbub around him. A large manila envelope was opened, a stack of papers beside it, and nothing would ever be the same again.

He could hear a couple of the new guys laughing with Hawk. They were just getting their feet on the ground, about to take HERO Force to the next level, and now they were going down. Crashing and burning like the goddamn Hindenburg.

He'd lived an interesting life and made more than his share of enemies over the years, but he never expected anything like this.

His cell phone rang.

Jax.

"You get one, too?" Cowboy asked.

"Yep. What are we going to do?"

Cowboy blew out air. "What the hell are our choices? We're guilty as fuck."

"Doesn't matter. We fight it, Leo. We fight it with everything we've got."

"As soon as the facts come out, HERO Force is done for anyway."

"Maybe. Maybe not."

Cowboy shook his head. "I love to agree with you, man, but you are living in a dream world if you think this is anything other than impending doom. If you and me were back in that shit storm again tomorrow, I'd do the same goddamn thing. But that doesn't make it right, and there ain't a court in the world that's going to let us get away with it."

"You might be right, but I'm not willing to let HERO Force and everything we've worked for get flushed down the shitter because of one misstep."

"This could go bad, Jax."

"It went bad a long time ago. Go home. Get some sleep. Kiss Charlotte for me."

"Yeah. And you kiss Jessa and that baby."

"It's going to be all right, Cowboy."

Cowboy hung up the phone. He wasn't so sure.

LOGAN'S HAVING AN AFFAIR WITH THE WOMAN IN CHARGE OF HERO FORCE'S FUTURE

Buy Justice for the SEAL

Sign up for Amy Gamet's mailing list
or text BOOKS to 66866

* * *

A note from Amy

Please take a moment to leave a review. Why? The number of reviews and their star-rating determine where I can advertise and promote my books. They also help other readers make purchasing decisions. I read every single review. Writing is solitary work, and feedback from readers puts a smile on my face and helps to counteract things like my kids calling me "the fun ender" and having to do laundry. (I really hate laundry.) If you're reading on a kindle, note that the "rate this book" feature at the end of an ebook is not the same as leaving a review. Only

Amazon sees those ratings and the stars have no effect on the star rating of the book.

This link will take you back to write a review at the retailer where you bought this book. Thank you so much for taking the time!

All the best,

Amy Gamet